Milo March is a har
James-Bondian charac
combination of person ... experience,
and intellect. He is a shrewd judge of human character, a crack shot, and a deeper character than I have found in most of the other spy/thriller novels I've read. But, above all, he is a con-man—and a very good one. It is Milo March himself who makes the series worth reading.

—Don Miller, *The Mystery Nook* fanzine 12

Steeger Books is proud to reissue twenty-three vintage novels and stories by M.E. Chaber, whose Milo March Mysteries deliver mile-a-minute action and breezily readable entertainment for thriller buffs.

Milo is an Insurance Investigator who takes on the tough cases. Organized crime, grand theft, arson, suspicious disappearances, murders, and millions and millions of dollars—whatever it is, Milo is just the man for the job. Or even the only man for it.

During World War II, Milo was assigned to the OSS and later the CIA. Now in the Army Reserves, with the rank of Major, he is recalled for special jobs behind the Iron Curtain. As an agent, he chops necks, trusses men like chickens to steal their uniforms, shoots point blank at secret police—yet shows compassion to an agent from the other side.

Whatever Milo does, he knows how to do it right. When the work is completed, he returns to his favorite things: women, booze, and good food, more or less in that order....

THE MILO MARCH MYSTERIES

Hangman's Harvest

No Grave for March

The Man Inside

As Old as Cain

The Splintered Man

A Lonely Walk

The Gallows Garden

A Hearse of Another Color

So Dead the Rose

Jade for a Lady

Softly in the Night

Uneasy Lies the Dead

Six Who Ran

Wanted: Dead Men

The Day It Rained Diamonds

A Man in the Middle

Wild Midnight Falls

The Flaming Man

Green Grow the Graves

The Bonded Dead

Born to Be Hanged

Death to the Brides

The Twisted Trap: Six Milo March Stories

A Lonely Walk

KENDELL FOSTER CROSSEN
Writing as
M.E. CHABER

With an Afterword by
KENDRA CROSSEN BURROUGHS

STEEGER BOOKS / **2020**

PUBLISHED BY STEEGER BOOKS
Visit steegerbooks.com for more books like this.

The unabridged novel has been lightly edited by Kendra Crossen Burroughs.

PUBLISHING HISTORY

Magazine
As "The Bodies Beautiful of Rome," *Cavalier*, July 1957 (vol. 5, no. 49), pp. 44–47, 59–77. Illustrated by Bob Schulze. A condensed version.

Hardcover
New York: Rinehart & Co., October 1956.
Toronto: Clarke, Irwin & Co., 1956.
London: T. V. Boardman (American Bloodhound Mystery #177), 1957.

Paperback
New York: Ace Double #D-225, 1957. Cover by Rudy Nappi. (Back-to-back with *Loser by a Head* by Harry Giddings.)
New York: Paperback Library (63-1421), A Milo March Mystery, #12, September 1970. Cover by Robert McGinnis.

ISBN: 978-1-61827-508-0

For Martha:

Omnia vincit Amor.
—Virgil

And for so many:

E lascia pur grattar dov'è la rogna.
—Dante

CONTENTS

AUTHOR'S NOTE

This is a story of the Rome of today, or tomorrow, but in the same way, although offered as a tale of melodrama and suspense, it is a story about you and me. What happened to Anna Maria Pericoloso and Riccardo Balena and Milo March could happen to us. Because of this, there are many real things in this novel, many real people, and many real places—and I hope much reality. The rest, while no less real in one sense, is the result of the author's imagination. Aside from those characters who appear under the names by which you know them from your daily newspaper, none of the characters is meant to portray any person living or dead.

M.E.C.

BEFORE THE BEGINNING ...

The beach was quiet in the night. There were miles of white sand, turned silver by the moonlight. The waves of the ocean were gentle with the hour of sleep, washing softly over the sand. The country slept—except for those who were a part of the night—except for those who used the night as a blanket to cover deeds that were better left unspoken and undone.

The car huddled against the rim of the road. They carried their burden across the sand toward the ocean. Their feet sank into the sand, the grains spilling into their shoes so that they cursed softly to themselves. They did not worry about tracks, for there had been many feet at the beach that day, but they were not accustomed to sand in their shoes. It made them uncomfortable. They were men of the night—but of the closed night where the floors were hard and the walls solid.

A few feet from the water, they placed her on the sand. Her face was up, and as they drew away, the moonlight brushed its silver over her bare body—over the breasts, firmer now in death, over the gentle sloping belly and over the loins that would never again writhe in passion. No matter what was to come after, this was her first funeral, and the soft light from the moon did well by her.

They started to leave, and their feet kicked up little spurts of sand so that some of the golden grains spilled on her breasts. One of the men turned back to brush the sand away. He liked everything to be clean and orderly and systematic.

ONE

The man made one last dab with his brush at the sign on the door and quit. He gathered up his brushes and his paint, grunted at me, and left. I stood in the corridor for a minute, just admiring the sign: *March's Insurance Service Corp.*

That's me. The name's Milo March. I'm an insurance investigator. Or insurance detective, if you like the word better. Which means that I get everything thrown at me that cops do—plus what the cops throw—without getting much of the credit. But the pay is better.

This was my first try on my own. I'd been working for an outfit in Denver, Colorado, for years. Finally, I'd gotten fed up with taking orders and making some other guy's bank account fat. Most of the insurance companies knew me, and several of them said they'd throw me some work. I moved to New York and took a little office on Madison Avenue, deep in the heart of the Martini Belt. A private office and a reception room and enough furniture to get by, including an empty filing cabinet. The man had just finished painting the name on the door and I was open for business. As soon as I made a couple of cases, I'd hire a receptionist. Blond and well stacked. At least, the view would be good on dull days.

I went into the office and sat behind the desk, trying to feel like an executive. It didn't work. I said to hell with it and opened the bottom drawer. There was a bottle of Canadian Club and some paper cups there for an emergency. Not feeling like an executive was an emergency. I poured myself a drink and sipped it, wondering how long I'd have to wait and if my bank account would hold out. I'd sent out cards with my address and phone number two days earlier.

The phone rang.

I snatched my hand back from the receiver and let it ring twice more before I picked it up.

"March's Insurance Service Corporation," I said, trying it on for size. It felt a little heavy.

"Milo?" a man asked.

"Yeah," I said. That sounded more natural.

"Martin Raymond," he said. "Congratulations, boy."

"Thanks," I said, trying to sound polite. Martin Raymond was a big wheel at Intercontinental Insurance Company. I'd worked for them a number of times and I'd sent him notice of my new setup.

"I think I might have a job for you, if you can handle it," he said.

"I guess I can," I said casually. "There are a couple of things on the fire, but there's always room for one more. What's the case?"

"How about running over here, boy, and I'll sketch it out for you."

I had to resist the impulse to drop the phone and start running immediately.

"Okay," I said. "I sent the girl out for something. As soon as she gets back, I'll be right over."

"Roger," he said and hung up.

I had another nip of the Canadian Club for luck. Then I locked the office and left. Intercontinental was about ten blocks away. I decided to walk so I wouldn't get there too quickly.

Intercontinental had been one of the first insurance companies to move uptown.

They owned their own building on upper Madison Avenue. They were one of the big companies, and I was feeling pretty good about the call. If Martin Raymond wanted to, he could throw me enough business to keep me going most of the time.

The reception room was big and glossy. A lot of policy payments had gone into furnishing it. There was a redhead at the reception desk who looked as if she'd been custom-built, like the furniture. I liked her lines better. I told her who I was, and a few minutes later I was on my way back to the inner sanctum.

Martin Raymond was pretty custom-built himself. He looked like a dozen other vice-presidents. His clothes came from Brooks Brothers. His accent came from Harvard. His hair was prematurely gray. You could tell by looking at him that, according to the fashion of the moment, he would always have a Bloody Mary, an extra dry martini, or something-on-the-rocks. Raymond might like some other drink, but he'd always order whatever the other vice-presidents were drinking, just as he'd always buy the right sort of tie.

"Glad to see you, Milo," he said as I came in. He gave me a manly, executive-type handshake. "Getting settled down in the big city?"

"Yeah," I said.

"Good boy. You know, I'm glad you decided to open up for yourself here. We used to send a lot of cases out to Denver just because we knew you'd be working on them."

"Thanks," I said. I suddenly realized that this was the second time I'd thanked him. I'd better watch that or he'd think there was something wrong with me.

"Your passport in order?"

"Yeah," I said. I tried not to look too interested. If he was interested in my passport, it meant a trip abroad—and a fat fee.

"How about your vaccination?"

"I was in Germany only a few months ago," I said, "so it's still good. Is Intercontinental handing out all-expense tours these days?"

"We are this time," he said. "Wrap this one up quickly and maybe we'll do it more often."

"What's the pitch?" I asked. "I thought you usually had the European stuff handled over there."

"We did," he said, "but I can't say we've ever been very happy about it. Our branch offices have always handled any investigations, but most of the time it's only meant that we paid the full freight. I've been wanting to make some other arrangements, and then your card and this case came in at the same time. We'll try it this once and see what happens."

"Must be a big one."

He shrugged. "Not so big. Life insurance. Twenty thousand dollars, with a double indemnity clause. Maybe you can save us the extra twenty thousand."

"Twenty thousand here and twenty thousand there," I said. "So somebody got knocked off and the local cops say it was an accident?"

"It's trickier than that," he said. "How's your Italian?"

"L'uccello vede il calamaio del professore sulla tavola," I said.

"What's that mean?"

"The bird sees the professor's inkwell on the table," I said. "It's the kind of thing they teach you, but I'm damned if I've ever found a good place to use it. Otherwise, I may be a little rusty, but it should come back to me. I was in Italy with the OSS some years back. What's the case?"

"A girl named Anna Maria Pericoloso. In Rome. Twenty-five years old. Her family's one of the group that's been making money since the war. They insured her for twenty thousand about two years ago. Double indemnity clause. They put in a claim for the full forty thousand dollars a week ago."

"How'd she die?"

"She was found early in the morning on the beach between Ostia and Torvaianica. In other words, about thirty miles south of Rome. She was lying there without any clothes on. She'd been dead for several hours."

"Drowned?"

"Who the hell knows," he said. For once he lost the Harvard accent. He sounded more like P.S. 41. "Luigi Manzo, our man in Rome, says he hasn't been able to get any information out of the cops. The case was closed in three days. The police and the girl's family say that she hadn't been feeling too well and that she had some idea that bathing in sea water made her feel better. They guess—guess, mind you—that she went down there at night to bathe in the nude, had a cramp when she was wading out, and drowned. Then the guess goes that the waves washed her back up on the beach."

"What bothers you about it?" I asked.

"Everything. For one thing, they never found her clothes. If she went swimming, then where are her clothes?"

"Hanging on a hickory limb," I said. "Anything else?"

"Luigi Manzo says that all Rome is buzzing with rumors about the case. He says that it has all the earmarks of being another Wilma Montesi case—she was even found only ten miles from where the other girl's body was found. Anyway, there's talk about politics, and that somebody high in the government caused the police to close the case. There's more talk about traffic in drugs and wild parties. The names of a couple of deported American gangsters have been dragged in. And there are others who think the family hired someone to kill her so they could collect the insurance. Oh, there are plenty of reasons for us to look into it."

"Maybe," I said. "It's not going to do you any good to prove murder unless you can prove somebody in the family did it."

"Of course," he said. "The results don't hang on whether you save us the extra twenty or not. You know how it is, Milo. We have to be on top of the heap all the time. Let somebody get away with something, even if it doesn't cost us any money, and soon everybody thinks he can get away with everything. We want you to go over there and shake it down for whatever is there. If it costs us forty, okay; if we save the twenty, double okay. But that's the way it is."

"Okay," I said. "I just wanted it put on the line. I'll take the job. One hundred a day and expenses."

"Right," he said.

"When do you want me to leave?" I asked.

He grinned at me. "Tomorrow. I have reservations for you on the Pan American leaving tomorrow."

"Pretty sure of yourself," I said.

He shrugged. "It figures, boy. You just opened. You can't have that much business already. We've got plenty to offer; you'll take it. It's all in the book."

"Someday," I said sourly, "you're going to run into something that isn't in the book and then you're going to have trouble. You'll have to turn in your charcoal-gray suit and untwist the lemon peel in your martini."

He laughed. "You're sharp today, boy. On your way out, stop and see my secretary. She'll give you your ticket and some expense money. Don't spend it all in one place."

That was pretty clear. I was back to being one of the hired help and he had other things to do. I stood up. "You want interim reports?" I asked.

He waved his hand. "At transatlantic phone rates?" he said. "I'll take the final report. I know you'll do right by us. On your way, boy. Give my love to those Italian film actresses."

"Sure, I will," I said. I went out and saw his secretary. She gave me a big fat envelope. I waited until I got out of the office to open it. Inside there was a round-trip ticket on Pan American and one thousand dollars in nice crisp bills. They were as lovely-looking as anything I'd seen in a long time.

I spent the rest of the afternoon getting ready to leave. I

arranged for a phone answering service to take all my calls. I knew an investigator at one of the insurance companies who promised to try to handle any cases for me that might come in, just so I wouldn't lose a client by not being there. Everything else I turned over to my attorney, Dick Jablow,* to handle.

The next day at about noon I was on the Pan American Clipper, watching the Long Island shoreline drop away beneath me. It was a seventeen-hour flight. I ate and drank and slept and tried to pretend that I didn't hear the roar of the motors. At eleven o'clock the following morning we landed in Rome. A coach took us into the air terminal at the railway station. From there I took a taxi to the Bernini Hotel on Piazzi Barberini. I had stayed there when I'd been in Rome before and liked it.

I checked in and went up to my room. I'd decided I was going to rest before I did anything—I'd never liked sleeping on planes. Everything in Rome would close up at one o'clock anyway, so it would be four or five before I could sit down with the Intercontinental man.

I had a bottle of Italian brandy sent up to the room. I had a couple of drinks out of it, then I took a shower. After that I had another drink and stretched out across the bed.

I was about two-thirds asleep when the phone rang. I came up out of it and grabbed the receiver.

"Pronto," I said.

---

* Since Dick Jablow does not appear in any other Milo March novel, I suspect that this may have been Ken Crossen's actual attorney at the time. Richard B. Jablow had many literary clients, according to his 1975 obituary in the *New York Times*. I noticed in other books of the series a few characters of this type, seemingly inserted into the story purely for the author's and his friends' amusement. (All footnotes were added by the editor.)

"Hello, Milo," a voice said in English. There was something vaguely familiar about it.

That took the rest of the sleep out of my eyes. So far as I knew, Luigi Manzo was the only person in Rome who knew I was coming, and even he didn't know what hotel I was going to stay at. Also, he had never met me and wasn't apt to be calling me by my first name.

"Who's this?" I asked.

He laughed. "Johnny Fornessi," he said.

I guess he knew he didn't need to ask if I remembered him. I knew him, all right. Johnny Fornessi was one of the American gangsters who had been deported to Italy. I'd brushed up against him a couple of times in the States and once in Italy after he'd been sent back. Nothing serious, but the brushes had been enough for us to know each other.

"How'd you know I was here and where I was staying?" I asked.

He laughed again, but there was no amusement or humor in it. There never was in Johnny Fornessi's laughter. "You know how it is," he said. "Word gets around. And whenever there's any word, I usually hear it. This place is a real Hickville, but I've started getting a few lines out."

"I'll bet," I said. "Don't tell me you've started a Welcome Neighbor movement?"

"No."

"Just wanted to hear the voice of an old pal?"

"Don't make me laugh."

"Okay," I said. "Then I give up. I was never any good at guessing games. I always did better with spin the bottle—but then you're the wrong type to play that with."

"Don't try to be funny," he said. "I called you because I want to do you a favor."

"Don't point it at me," I said. "Your favors are always loaded."

"I figured you might misunderstand," he said, "but I'll take the chance. I ain't got no interest in this myself, but I don't like to see another American knocked off if it can be helped."

"Or unless you can do the knocking off," I said. "You interest me, Johnny. Who's going to do all this to me?"

"I don't know," he said. "Honest, I don't, Milo. All I heard was that you were coming over here to work on the death of the Pericoloso girl. The way I hear it, there are a lot of important people who want it left alone."

"There are always people who want things left alone," I said. "You know me, Johnny. I don't scare that easily."

"Meaning you're going ahead with it?"

"Bright boy," I said. "Want to try for the sixty-four thousand dollars?"

"You're the one who's trying," he said. "You're going for the thirty-two caliber question." There was a click as he hung up.

TWO

I put the receiver back on the hook. I poured myself a drink and sipped it slowly. One thing was sure. I couldn't complain of being neglected. The only question was why. I knew Johnny Fornessi. He'd been a big wheel back in the States. He'd represented the Syndicate and the Mafia on the West Coast. Then he and his right-hand man, a little gunman named Lucky Topo, had been deported. The rumor was that Johnny still had a lot to do with crime back in the States. The question was, why was he interested in a girl who was supposed to have taken a lonely walk along a beach and died? The insurance money was too small to attract Johnny Fornessi. There had to be something else in it.

He'd said he was doing it as a friendly gesture. I didn't go for that bit. Johnny never had any friends. If he did, he wouldn't do anything for them unless there was a buck in it.

Finally I gave up and went back to sleep. It was almost four when I awakened. I got dressed and left the hotel. The Intercontinental office was on Via Sistina, and that was just around the corner from the hotel. I walked.

The office was barely open. A sleepy-eyed, olive-skinned girl was in the reception room. She looked at me questioningly as I entered.

"Signor Luigi Manzo, per piacere," I said. *"Mi chiamo Milo March."*

A look of intelligence came over her face, so I guessed that Intercontinental had told the office I was coming. She picked up the phone and passed along the information that I was there. She put the phone down and told me to go through the door on the other side of her desk.

As I went through the door, a short, heavyset man came around the desk with outstretched hand and a big grin. He had black curly hair and dark olive skin. He looked to be in his middle thirties.

"Mi chiamo Luigi Manzo," he said. *"Piacere di conoscerti."*

"Lei è molto gentile," I said.

"Ah," he said, his face fighting up, "you speak my language beautifully. How is that? Come and sit down."

"I was here during the war," I explained as I took the chair next to his desk.

He looked at me curiously. "Before the occupation?"

"Yeah," I said. "Before the invasion. It was an informal visit."

He grinned broadly. "Good. Then you are just the man for this business—if anything is to be done about it."

I gave him a cigarette, and lit his and mine. "Which reminds me. I suppose Intercontinental's New York office told you I was coming?"

"Certainly," he said.

"When?"

"The cablegram arrived early this morning."

"Who else knew about it besides you?"

"The girl, naturally," he said. "She opens all business communications and places them on my desk. Why?"

"Did you tell anyone I was coming?"

He shook his head.

"How about the girl? Think she might tell someone?"

He threw up his hands. "I suppose she might mention to a girlfriend that an American was coming, certainly no more than that. I will ask her." He picked up the phone and put the question to the girl. He listened a minute and replaced the receiver. "She says that she told no one. I am inclined to believe her. Now, why is this, Signore?"

"You know the name Johnny Fornessi?" I asked.

He nodded. "Everyone in Rome knows the name. He is one of our mistakes which you Americans shipped back to us. I have heard one whisper that he knows something about the murder of Anna Maria Pericoloso."

"He certainly knows about whispers," I said. "I had barely checked into my hotel—and no one knew where I was going to be staying—when Johnny called me and told me to lay off this case."

He swore beneath his breath. "Then he must be involved. How did he find out where you were staying?"

"That would be easy. The question is, how did he know that I was coming? Once he knew that, he could have someone waiting to follow me as soon as I landed. Well, to hell with him. What about this case?"

He spread his hands in a gesture of futility. "I have sent the company everything I know. The girl died three weeks ago. The parents put in a claim a week ago. Everything seemed proper. The parents said that she'd gone down to the beach very early to bathe in the ocean because she hadn't been feeling well. Both the family doctor and the police said that her death was accidental. Everything seemed in order. But as I gathered this meager information, the whispers kept occurring."

"What kind of whispers?" I asked. "From where? Who whispered?"

He shrugged. "You must understand, Signore, that Rome is a city of whispers. It goes on all the time, whispers about politics, the love lives of the great, anything. One learns to ignore it. Perhaps the first one came from a clerk in the Interior Ministry, perhaps the casual remark of a friend. Later I heard talk in the wineshops. Nothing you could pin down, you understand."

"All right," I said impatiently. "What were the whispers?"

"That the girl was murdered, that she had been at a drug party with important people and had been left on the beach to die, that she was pregnant and the guilty man could not stand the scandal. It was said that many important people were involved and the police had hushed everything up. It is still being said."

"Any names?"

He smiled. "There are always names in the whispers of Rome. This Johnny Fornessi was one mentioned. It is said that he is not as retired as he seems. Then the whispers mention the names of Baron Mario Gambero and Riccardo Balena, the son of the Minister of the Interior."

"That's all?" I asked.

"It is enough."

"I guess it is," I admitted. "Who's Baron Gambero?"

"A man of influence," he said. "It has always been so. Before the war, he was an important *fascista.* It is believed that now he is one of the *fascisti fanatici,* although he does not openly belong to their party. He is friendly with many men in the government. There are also many whispers about him—one of them being that he is in business with Johnny Fornessi."

"Sounds like a cozy little situation," I said. "What did you do about the whispers, besides mail them to the office?"

"Nothing." He spread his hands again. "I tried. But the police would do nothing except give me the statement that it was accidental death and the case was closed."

"According to your report, the girl's clothes were never found?"

"That is true. I asked the police, but they would tell me nothing. It is possible that you, being an American, will be treated with more respect by them."

"Maybe," I said. I didn't have any hopes that the police anywhere would treat an insurance detective with respect. "How about other aspects of the whispers? Did you ask around about them?"

He hesitated. "It is not wise for a businessman in Rome to inquire too deeply into such matters. I will confess to you, Signore, a certain amount of fear, but that is not the only reason. I think that this is a most explosive matter."

"Is there any other kind?" I asked, grinning. "But I don't blame you. That's not what you're hired for. I guess the best place for me to start is with the police. If I'm going to be thrown out, it might as well be by somebody with authority."

He laughed. "I will go with you if you wish, although I cannot do anything to help you there, Signor March."

"Call me Milo," I said. I looked at him for a minute. "No reason for you to come along. Maybe I'll do better if I just stumble around like a dumb American. I'll keep in touch."

"A rivederci," he said. "If there's anything I can do ..."

"Sure," I said, and left.

On the way out, still wondering how anyone had found out I was coming, I stopped beside the reception desk. The girl who sat there busily typing looked to be in her middle thirties. She had black hair pulled severely back around her head to form a bun. Her face was typically Italian and might have been beautiful if it had not been set in such severe lines. She wore heavy glasses, which didn't do anything for her either. She wore an almost shapeless dress, so it was impossible to tell what her body was like. Probably overly heavy.

She finally stopped working and looked up. She stared at me blankly.

"Hello," I said. "What's your name?"

"Wilma Pianta," she said.

"I just wanted to get acquainted," I said. "I'll probably be around for a few days. I'm from the New York office of Intercontinental. My name is Milo March."

"I know," she said.

"Oh, yes, I told you when I came in, didn't I?"

"I knew who you were before that," she said.

"How?"

She looked as if she were sorry she had started it. "From—from the time you were here just before the war."

"The underground?" I said. "You were in it?"

She nodded.

"Where?"

"Here in Rome."

That was the section in which I'd worked and I'd known, or known of, everybody in the underground. Or thought I had. "And your name is Wilma Pianta?"

"Yes." Her voice was so low I could hardly hear her. "But I wasn't known by my name then."

"What were you called?"

"La Ragazza."

La Ragazza. The Girl. I remembered that name. I'd never seen her, but I'd heard of her—as anyone had who was in Italy at that time. She was a young, beautiful girl—well, I guess she would have been more beautiful in those times. She had been the scourge of the Fascists and the Nazis. I remembered that it had been said she had accounted for more of them than any other single member of the underground.

"I'm sorry," she was saying. "I didn't intend to mention it."

I knew what she meant. I had been about to say something about being surprised to find La Ragazza working as a receptionist in an insurance office, but it seemed pretty pointless. I was working for the same insurance company. And I knew how she felt about even mentioning it. It had been an obscene period. I knew that. I'd cut plenty of throats then myself.

It was hardly the time for cutting up old touches. "It's okay," I told her. Now it also seemed pretty silly even vaguely to suspect her of selling office secrets. "It was a pretty rough period. I know how you feel. Well—I'll be seeing you."

She looked up and smiled at me as I left. It was a pretty smile.

Downstairs, I took a taxi to police headquarters. It was a big, square building on Via Milano. I went in and told them I wanted to see someone in authority. I showed my passport, my identification from Intercontinental, and everything but my vaccination scar. After I'd gone through this four times I was finally shown in to a man who assured me that he was most anxious to be of assistance to Americans. I told him that I was equally anxious to be of assistance to Italians. We continued with this little formal dance until we both ran out of adjectives.

"Now," he said finally, "what can I do for my distinguished colleague from America?"

"I hate to bother you with the small matters of my business," I said, "but I am interested in the death of Anna Maria Pericoloso."

Something about the way his eyes flickered told me that he knew the name well.

But he wasn't going to walk into that one.

"Pericoloso," he murmured. "I'm not sure it is familiar. Perhaps you could locate it more definitely for me."

"Sure," I said. "The girl was found dead on the beach near Ostia about three weeks ago. I believe the theory was that she'd gone swimming for reasons of health."

He was still giving me the poker face. "I am not familiar with all the things which pass through here," he said apologetically. "Just a moment ..."

He picked up the phone and asked someone to bring him

anything they had on Pericoloso, Anna Maria. Then he turned back to me and told me again how much he loved America. He managed to keep this up until a policeman came in and handed him a folder. I noticed that the folder was pretty thin.

He opened it and pretended to read, but I could tell he wasn't actually reading. Finally, he looked up and smiled. "Yes, Signor March, that seems to be correct. Apparently the young lady wasn't feeling well and went for a swim about four o'clock in the morning. Her family have stated that she often did this. Apparently she suffered a cramp or some such mishap and drowned. She was found on the beach that morning. Most unfortunate. What did you say your interest in the matter was?"

"I didn't say. But the company I represent carried a life insurance policy on her for twenty thousand dollars, forty thousand dollars in the event of accidental death."

"Ah," he said. "I imagine that it will be welcomed by the family. They are not especially wealthy. You have come over to present the money to them?"

"Not exactly," I said. "There seems to be a little doubt that they will get the full amount."

"Who doubts it?"

"Me."

He managed to look surprised. *"Non capisco."*

"It's simple," I said. "I'm not sure that her death was accidental."

"Surely you joke," he said. "Drowning is hardly a natural death."

I thought it was time to bring it out in the open. "Neither is murder," I said.

He looked both surprised and alarmed, although he didn't want me to see the latter emotion. "But surely, Signore, the police of Italy—"

"I hold the police of Italy in the highest esteem," I said smoothly. "This is why I came directly to you. I'm sure you won't mind answering a few questions for me."

"Not at all," he said warily.

"First," I said, "who investigated the case for the police?"

He glanced at the report. "Detective Piero Roccia."

"Can I talk with him?"

He looked startled but quickly recovered. "I'm afraid that he is not on duty today. Perhaps another time, if you are in Rome long enough. ... But it should not be necessary, Signore. Everything is in the reports."

I thought he was lying, but there was no way I could prove it.

"Fine," I said. "The girl's body was found on the beach near Ostia?"

"Yes."

"How far from Rome?"

"A little more than twenty miles."

"I believe you said that she went there about four in the morning?"

"Yes."

"How did she go?" I asked casually.

He shrugged. "I imagine she drove herself. It is a short, pleasant drive."

"You found her car?" I asked.

He realized he'd walked into a trap, but he managed a

smile. "No," he said. "Now that you mention it, perhaps it is more likely that she took a taxi."

"Perhaps," I said politely. "I believe the report stated that the girl had been bathing in the nude?"

"Yes. It is not unusual for individuals to bathe in the nude below Ostia early in the morning. The girl's family stated that she often did this when she wasn't feeling well."

"Very healthy, I'm sure," I said. "Tell me, Signore, how near the body did you find the girl's clothes?"

That one caught him, too. He looked in the report, but obviously there was no help there. He began to lose some of his warmth.

"I do not know exactly," he said. "Perhaps she walked along the beach before going into the water ..."

"It must have been a lonely walk—until Death came to keep her company," I said. I grinned at him. "Did you find any of her clothing?"

"A person's clothing does not just vanish," he said with all the dignity he could muster. He closed the report with a definite air. "I am sorry, Signor March, that there is not more information to give you. But you must see that it was a routine accident, and in such cases we do not collect so much information. I am sorry that I cannot be of more assistance, but the case is closed. There is nothing more to be learned." He said it firmly.

The interview was over. I stood up and smiled again. "I understand," I said.

"I was certain you were a man of perception," he said. He was still being polite, but it was a strain. "The case is closed. I am sorry if this means your company will have to pay out money, but then that is the business they are in, is it not?"

"More or less," I admitted. "But sometimes it seems to me that a lot of people are in the business of paying out money—for one reason of another."

He got what I meant. His face got darker and his lips tightened. But that was the only sign he made. "When do you leave Rome, Signor March?"

"I don't know," I said. "To tell you the truth, I rather like it in Rome. I may even go down to Ostia and try the bathing—for my health, of course."

"Signor March," he said, and the politeness was gone from his voice, "the case is closed. The Italian police, unlike the police in your own country, do not welcome the ideas of every amateur who thinks he knows something. As a friend, I suggest that you see the tourist sights of Rome and then go quietly home."

I was beginning to get annoyed. "I've seen the sights of Rome," I told him quietly. "I saw them during the war—over the sights of a gun."

I turned and left. As I went through the door, he was picking up the phone.

Leaving, I had to go through a room where there were a number of men who I guessed to be detectives. There's something about detectives in any country that always gives them away. Maybe it's the fact that they wear suits as if they were costumed for a masked ball. One of the men was putting down the phone as I came into the room. From the way he looked up at me, I had a hunch that the phone call had been about me. From the man I'd just left.

I walked up to the group of men. "Piero Roccia around?" I asked.

It was the man who had been on the phone who answered me. Maybe I just had a suspicious nature, but it seemed he answered too quickly.

"No," he said. "Can I do something for you, Signore?"

"No," I said cheerfully. "I wanted to see Piero. My name is Milo March."

"Your business with him, Signore?"

"No business. I just remembered that I might know a cousin of his in Brooklyn. I'm staying at the Bernini Hotel, if he's interested." I went on without waiting for an answer.

Out on Via Milano I stopped and looked around. I wasn't sure where I was going next, but I knew I wasn't going to drop it now. Especially now. I lit a cigarette and thought about it.

I was still standing there when a small, dark man came out of the Ministry building. He was thin and wiry, looking a little the way George Raft did when he was young.* He came down the stairs without looking at me. I thought maybe he'd been sent out to tail me until he brushed past me.

"Avanti Caffè, two blocks from here," he said as he went by. He walked on down the street without looking back.

I waited a few minutes, then hailed a cab. I told the driver where I wanted to go. I also let him know that I was aware that it was only two blocks so he wouldn't waste time going

* The actor George Raft was known for playing tough guys in movies such as *Scarface* (1932) and was rumored to be a gangster in real life.

by the way of the Vatican. I leaned back and the cab drove off. This way it would look better if anyone was watching.

The cab stopped in front of the caffè. I paid the driver and got out. I went inside and looked around. The small, dark man was sitting at a table in the corner, apparently reading a paper he had taken from the rack. I went over to the table.

"Hello," I said.

"Sit down," he said. He looked at me with black, expressionless eyes. "I'm Piero Roccia."

"Milo March," I said. We shook hands. "You were in the room when I asked for you?"

He nodded. "I have taken the liberty of ordering coffee for both of us. I hope you don't mind. We will talk after we have been served."

"Okay," I said.

He continued to read the newspaper. A waiter came with a pot of coffee and cups. He plopped them on the table and left.

The detective folded the newspaper and put it aside. He poured coffee for both of us, then looked at me again.

"You are interested in the death of Anna Maria Pericoloso?" he asked.

I was surprised. "How did you know that's what I was interested in? I didn't mention it when I asked for you."

"And I have no cousins in Brooklyn," he answered with a smile. "I knew it quite by accident, Signore. I was in an office earlier this morning where a call was received. The message was that an American named Milo March would be in to ask about the Pericoloso case."

"Who called?" I asked.

"I was not told."

"You know Johnny Fornessi?"

"I know him."

"Could it have been he?"

"It could have been," he said slowly, "but I cannot say it was."

"When I stopped to ask for you," I said, "the man who answered me had just been told to keep me from seeing you, hadn't he?"

He nodded.

"Very interesting," I said. "You know, when I left New York yesterday, only one man in Rome knew that I was coming. He swears that he told no one. Even he did not know where I would be staying. But I was barely in my hotel before I received a call suggesting that I'd better forget my reason for coming here. Somebody calls the police and warns them I'll be there. Then the police tell me it might be healthier to go back to New York. What is even odder is that the police tell me that the detective who worked on the case in which I'm interested—named Piero Roccia—is not on duty when in fact he is. Could you explain this to me?"

"Perhaps," he said. He stared at me searchingly. "Signor March, what is your interest in the death of the girl?"

"She was insured by the company for which I work," I said. "If her death was accidental, they have to pay double. Naturally, they would like to save money, but something else is important to them. If there was anything peculiar about her death, they want to uncover it so that people won't get the idea that it's easy to put things over on them."

"That is your company," he said. "What about you?"

"I work for them," I said. "I know very little about the case at this point. I started out with nothing to make me think that the death was not accidental except vague rumors. I must confess that every minute I'm in Rome makes me more certain that there was nothing accidental in the girl's death."

"May I ask why you think this?"

"Mostly the threats and the treatment by the police. I confess that there are also two questions I'd like answered. I couldn't get an answer today. One, how did the girl get to the beach—and what happened to her means of transportation? Two, what happened to her clothes if she just went in for an innocent swim?"

He nodded thoughtfully and accepted one of my cigarettes. "I investigated the death of Anna Maria Pericoloso," he said. "From the beginning I was sure that she was murdered. With each step I became more certain, and when the case closed I was positive. This is why I am coming to you over my superiors' heads."

"Why?" I asked.

"Why am I doing this?" he asked. "I have been with the police since the end of the war, Signore, and I am proud of it. I am aware of what this afternoon has made you think. I hope you will not judge the Italian police by this. It is not a usual situation. What I am doing in talking to you is merely upholding a little of what I believe the police are and should be."

"I understand," I told him. "Actually I was asking why you were so convinced about the girl."

He nodded again. "Pardon me, Signor March," he said, "if

I at first seem cautious with you. But I do not know you. I do not know what sort of man you are or have been. You were in the war?"

"I was in it," I said. "I was right here in Rome when our armies marched in. I'd been here for three months."

"Ah," he said, "that tells me much about you. Tell me something else, Signor March. This afternoon you were told the case was closed and to leave it alone. You are an American, and as such you have few rights in my country in regard to the work you wish to do. If you persist, you will run into much more of this. You may not only be told by important Italians, you may even get orders from your own Embassy. You may find yourself arrested and in jail. You may find someone trying to kill you. All of these things may happen to you—if you say out loud that one unimportant girl died because someone wished her to die. What about this?"

"Do you mean will I take the first plane back to the States?" I asked. I laughed. "Piero, I've been around a long time. You can't work in insurance cases without frequently ruffling important people. I've been ordered out of places. I've been arrested. I've been shot at. It's a job—and I'm a stubborn man."

He reached across the table and shook my hand again. This time there was an impulsive warmth in his grip. "My feelings were right," he said. "When I saw you for the first time a few minutes ago, I thought that you were the man like myself. But I had to find out." He leaned back and produced cigarettes. "Signor March—"

"My name is Milo," I said. I took one of his cigarettes and held my lighter.

He smiled, his teeth flashing white in the dark face. "Milo, *amico,*" he said. "We will work well together. I have a feeling for this. There are things which make men what they are. Many Italians were opposed to the rule of Mussolini in theory, but very few went into the underground. I was in it from the time I began to think of myself as a man. Too many good Italians thought that all they had to do was wait for Mussolini to be finished. So they waited twenty years. And it softened them. Then the years before the war and during the war, there were many strange friendships. Today, there are still many good Italians who find themselves chained by things that happened long ago."

He paused and stared out of the window. I waited patiently. I knew that everything he was saying was important to him and that he'd get around to the girl in his own time. I sipped my coffee and waited.

"We Italians," he said, "are strange people. We are the most ardent Catholics in the world, but we look upon our priests as men and are apt to ignore them on many matters. There are many of us who go to Mass every morning and a Communist cell meeting every night and see nothing strange about it. Many of our cultural leaders sneer at America for publishing comic magazines, yet these very men have helped to flood Italy with the same thing. We put our women on a pedestal and keep them there, but *pappagallismo,* the sport of flirting, is a highly developed art. In the spring, we see nothing wrong with helping ourselves to a small pinch. Most foreigners misunderstand this. We Romans don't really go around pinching girls, but if we take a little pinch in the spring it is only because we are happy with the sun and the warm weather. We are filled with contradictions which are not contradictions if only you understand them."

I did understand what he was saying. "I know," I said. I laughed at a sudden memory. "Once when Mussolini's Black Shirts were looking for me, I became for a moment a member of *i pappagalli della strada.*"

"The parrots of the street," he repeated in delight.

"It was not only pleasant," I said, "but the *fascisti* did not give me a second glance."

"You see, even politics do not change certain things," he said. "The little pinch, the bold remark, under the proper circumstances it is the right thing—but were you to kiss a girl in public, the Good Custom Squad would arrest you and you would be fined three hundred lire."

"Forty-eight cents," I said. "It might be worth it."

He sighed heavily. "Perhaps we should get to work. ..."

"I suppose so," I admitted. "What can you tell me?"

"Not much that you don't know or have not guessed," he said. "I do not know how Anna Maria Pericoloso reached Ostia. If she drove herself, as has been suggested, then her car melted into the sand. I did not find a taxi driver who had been summoned. I was never able to find any of her clothes. Although it is not in the report, the doctor told me that she had been under the influence of drugs when she died. There was no autopsy, but if there had been, I think it would have proved an overdose of drugs—or that something else had been added to the drugs she took. I can swear to you that she had not been in the water that night and there was no water in her lungs when I saw her body—still on the beach where it was found. But this is not evidence, you understand."

"It's enough evidence for me at the moment," I said. "What about the rumors?"

He shrugged. "I can tell you this. South of Ostia, about twenty miles, is Torvaianica. Just outside of this village is the country estate of Baron Mario Gambero. For thirty years Baron Gambero has been a pimp, a panderer, a tax dodger, an opportunist, and the friend of the important. He was an important Fascist. During the war, he befriended many an enemy of Fascism. There are men in power today who owe their lives to him. The change in political faiths bothered him not at all. He always lands on his feet with his money firmly in his pockets."

"There are men like him in every country."

"True. Remember, now I tell you only facts. Gambero has all sorts of friends.

Giuseppe Formaggio, the head of Italian police, owes his life to Gambero. They are close friends. Formaggio is like your Signor Hoover.* The Italian police are part of the Ministry of the Interior. The present Minister of the Interior is Silvano Balena, who also owes his life to Gambero. They are friends. Gambero is also a good friend of the Minister's son, Riccardo Balena. The young man is a son of his times. He is wild. He gambles, he drinks, he uses drugs, he is a despoiler of women, he is interested only in jazz music, money, and what he considers good times. For a time he was the constant escort

* J. Edgar Hoover, longtime director of the FBI, was criticized for not going after organized crime. He even denied that the Mafia existed in the U.S., until 1957, which was after the publication of this book.

of Anna Maria Pericoloso. Some of these times, he escorted her to parties at Gambero's estate near Torvaianica."

"Interesting," I said.

He nodded. "Here is one more fact. On the morning of the third day after the death of the girl, Gambero drove into Rome. With him were Riccardo Balena and an actress named Gianna Bionda, who is said to have succeeded Anna Maria in the affections of young Balena. The young man and the girl sat in the car while Gambero went into the Ministry and visited with the senior Balena and Giuseppe Formaggio. That afternoon, the case on Anna Maria Pericoloso was officially closed."

"Is Gambero also a friend of Johnny Fornessi?" I asked.

"Oh, yes. Now, I have given you facts, and we come to rumors. It is said that Gambero also makes a practice of going in business with the sons of important men. Any business. It is said that Gambero is a secret partner of Johnny Fornessi in drugs and that the country estate is the seat of operations. No evidence has ever been secured. It is whispered that Riccardo Balena had a date with Anna Maria that night before she died and that there was a party at the estate. It is said that the girl knew too much and that if Riccardo were to drop her she was going to talk. It is variously said that Gambero himself killed her, that Riccardo killed her, that Johnny Fornessi did it. I have also heard that Gambero has said that his young friend was in serious trouble and he had saved the boy's neck."

"What do you think?" I asked.

"Only that a small truth lies somewhere in all this," he said simply. "But my hands are now tied and I cannot do anything. Something should be done—but most carefully."

"Meaning what?"

"Milo," he said seriously, "this is not only the matter of the life of a young girl—although that is enough reason to be aroused. There is much in this that is explosive. So far there are only whispers. But whispers in Rome cannot be controlled. Soon they will find their way into print. The Communists will grab them. The Socialists will grab them. So will the Monarchists and the Movimento Sociale Italiano. It could be the end of Italian democracy. With the whispers, it is already too late to forget the case even if one wanted to. Any minute it will be broken wide open. The murder of Anna Maria must not only be solved, it must be solved quickly."

"I can see that," I said.

"It can only be solved quickly," he said, "by a man who will not be frightened or bluffed by anyone. Are you this man?"

"You're giving me a big load," I told him.

Once more he shrugged. "We will see," he said. "In the meantime, I will give you what little help I can. It will not be much. I have the name of a man you can yet see this afternoon. I think he can tell you many things. He is a professional informer, although not too many know this. His information is for sale, but not for money only. If he does not feel that he is dealing with a man of courage, he will not sell for any price. Go see him."

I nodded.

"His name is Attilio Coniglio. There is a little wineshop called Martello on Via Maria Cristina, near the river. Attilio will be there within the half hour. He goes there every day. Tell him that I sent you to him."

"Right," I said.

"Tonight," he said, "I will come to your hotel. We will have dinner together and I think I can show you some of the people involved. I cannot arrange for you to meet them—although perhaps I can in one case. But you should know what they look like."

"Okay. I'll see you tonight."

"Good." He stood up. "The coffee is on my bill, so don't worry about the account. *Buona fortuna.*"

"I'll need it," I murmured as he left. I waited a few minutes, lighting a cigarette and thinking about the case. I couldn't really complain that nothing had happened since I landed in Rome a few hours earlier. Finally, I got up and left.

There was a taxi parked a couple of doors from the caffè. I walked over to it and opened the door. Only then did I become aware that somebody was sitting in the back seat.

"Scusi," I said and started to close the door.

"Don't rush it, Milo," a familiar voice said. "I've been waiting for you. I feel it ain't nice for me to let a fellow American run around without anybody to show him the sights. Get in."

It was Johnny Fornessi. The gun in his hand was held loosely, but still it pointed at me.

THREE

There wasn't much choice. I didn't want to be impolite, so I got into the cab and sat next to him. The cab started up at once. I couldn't see anything of the driver except the back of his head. I turned to look at Johnny. He looked pretty much the same as when I last saw him before he was deported. Johnny Fornessi had always suggested the idea that someone had tried to make a well-dressed, good-looking, honest man and had just missed. Johnny wasn't quite well dressed, not quite good-looking, and certainly not honest, and that was what you saw when you looked at him.

"You heeled, Milo?" he asked. He didn't wait for an answer but leaned over and patted me in the places where a gun might be carried. He shook his head when he didn't find one. "You slipping, Milo? No gun. A man can get hurt that way."

"Sometimes they can get hurt even when they carry one," I said evenly.

"Not me, sweetheart," he said. He slipped his gun inside his coat. "I'll put it away, but don't try anything, Milo. I still know how to use it."

"You planning on using it?" I asked.

"Not unless you make me."

"Okay, then, what's the idea of the cowboy-and-Indian act?"

"Like I said, I figured it was a shame to have you just wandering around Rome. I'm going to show you the sights."

"Starting with Ostia?" I asked.

He ignored the question. He was looking out the window, and sure enough he started telling me what buildings we were passing. It was so fascinating hearing this New York gangster reeling off the facts about the Giuseppe Mazzini monument and the Cloaca Massima that for several minutes I listened instead of trying to figure out what was going on.

"Johnny, you surprise me," I said finally. "You've got all the patter down."

"Yeah," he said. "When I first came back to this joint, it took me a while to make any connections. I saw every damn part of this town maybe fifteen or twenty times."

"What about the prisons?"

"Not Johnny Fornessi," he said, and his old arrogance was back in his voice.

"I guess sightseeing isn't a problem now," I said. "I hear you've got good connections. Like Gambero."

"I got connections," he said.

"Is that why you're interested in the Pericoloso girl, Johnny? Or did you kill her?"

"Never heard of her," he said. He went back to telling me the sights and brushed off any other attempts on my part to start a conversation.

We crossed the river and swung over past Vatican City, then by a lot of palaces, one of which Johnny said had been occupied by Mussolini's mistress. We crossed the river again. I glanced at my watch and saw that we'd been riding around for an hour. Johnny must have noticed the time then, too, for he suddenly dropped the chatter.

"All right, Milo," he said. "You want us to take you back to your hotel?"

"You mean it's over?" I asked. "Just as I was beginning to enjoy it, too. I was even looking forward to a guided tour of Baron Gambero's country estate. I hear the air is very stimulating there."

"Don't be a wise guy," he snapped. "Where do you want to go?"

I still wanted to go to the wineshop. I knew it was near the river and we had just crossed the river.

"Make it right here," I said.

He looked surprised. "What's right here?"

"A good place to leave you. You bore me, Johnny. Besides, after riding with you for an hour, I'm not sure you've had a bath recently."

His face darkened with anger. He rapped out one word at the driver and the cab swerved to the curb.

"Just one thing, Milo," he said as I started to get out. "I know you. You're a pretty tough guy, but you're trying to play in the wrong league. It's too fast for you. Play it smart and take the next plane back to the States."

"And miss the chance to meet a real, live baron?" I said, wide-eyed. "How could I go back and face the boys in the poolroom if I did that?"

"Okay," he said. "Just remember I tried to warn you. I'll be seeing you, Milo."

I got out of the car, then turned back, still holding the door open. "You've made your speech, Johnny," I said. "Now I think I'll make one. You've been pushing. I don't like it. I'm going to be around, but I'm not sure you'll be seeing me—or anything else." I slammed the door as hard as I could.

I stood on the sidewalk until they'd driven out of sight. Then I hailed a cab and told the driver to take me to the Martello wineshop on Via Maria Cristina.

It was a short drive. The cab pulled up in front of a little cellar place with a picture of a hammer in front of it.* I paid the driver and got out. There was a car parked in front, but I didn't pay any attention. I walked down a short flight of steps to the front door. That was as far as I got. A uniformed policeman stood there, barring my way.

"The wineshop is not open now," he announced.

"Why not?" I asked.

"There has been a murder, Signore."

I guess I started getting it then, even before he told me. "Who was killed?"

He shrugged. "Some informer. He was stabbed in the throat as he sat drinking wine. It is to be expected with such people."

"And the murderer?" I asked tightly.

"Nobody saw the crime, and the murderer was gone before we were called. But the police will get him, Signore, you may be sure of that."

"Yeah," I said. I turned and walked up to the sidewalk. For a minute I thought I was going to be sick, but I finally fought it down. Now I knew why Johnny had taken me sightseeing, but I couldn't see how he knew it was necessary. Unless

* Martello, the name of the shop, means "hammer" in Italian.

the detective … but that didn't make sense. I gave it up and walked to the corner. I hailed a cab and went back to the hotel.

There were messages at the desk that Signor Manzo had phoned twice and Signor Marrone had called once. I couldn't remember knowing anyone named Marrone. I went up to my room. Part of the bottle of brandy was still there. I had them send up some ice. Then I had two stiff drinks and felt a little better. I picked up the phone and called police headquarters. I asked for Piero Roccia. Somebody answered, but it didn't sound like him. I asked for him again.

"Who is calling?" the man asked.

"His Uncle Umberto," I snapped.

Finally he came on the phone.

"This your Uncle Umberto from Brooklyn," I said. "I hope your line isn't tapped."

"No," he said.

"You know about the killing?"

"Yes."

"I was kept away for an hour by an old friend. Johnny Fornessi."

"You want to do something about it?" he asked.

"I will," I said. "In my own way. I'm sure there's no point in charging him. He probably has fourteen alibis. But if I were the police, I'd check him and that little pal of his, Lucky Topo. Just for luck. You won't find anything."

"You're probably right."

"Will I still see you tonight?" I asked.

"Yes."

"Okay," I said. "Now I want a favor. I've been here less than twelve hours. Everybody seems to know my business. Johnny Fornessi knew I was coming and where I was staying. Somebody knew I was coming to the police. Somebody knew you were sending me to a wineshop, and a man died with a knife in his throat while I was being forced to look at museums. I'm being pushed around. I don't like it. I want a gun."

"You mean that you want a permit?" he asked.

"I don't give a damn how," I said. "Legal or illegal. I want a gun. Can you do something for me?"

"I think so," he said carefully. "Wait until I see you tonight. I'll be there in a little more than an hour."

"Okay," I said, and hung up.

I had another drink and then I called the Intercontinental office. Wilma Pianta answered the phone. She sounded breathless, the way a woman will when she's been hanging on the phone waiting for it to ring.

"Oh, Signor March," she said. "Signor Manzo tried to reach you several times. He was worried about not hearing from you. When he hadn't heard by the time we normally close the office, he asked me to stay so there would be someone here if you did phone."

So that was why she sounded breathless; she'd had to stay overtime and had probably been cursing me every minute I was late.

"I'm sorry," I told her. "I didn't even realize that he was expecting me to call. I'll tell him not to make you stay around in the future."

"Oh, I don't mind, Signor March," she said. "I am grateful for the opportunity to help you and Signor Manzo."

I knew, as she spoke, that she was undoubtedly telling the truth. And I could understand it. She'd been raised in an Italy that had been right out of a dime novel. She'd grown up on excitement, and now she was crowding middle age and the most exciting thing in her life was typing a dull report in triplicate. Just sitting on the phone and hearing about things would be an adventure. I'd feel the same way if I were chained to a desk.

"Nothing has happened," I told her. There was no point in telling her or Manzo that a man had died because he was willing to carry tales. "If you know where I can reach him, I'll call and put his mind at rest. Or would you rather call him?"

"I'll call him for you," she said eagerly. "He—he was wondering if you had any plans. That is, that you would care to tell him about."

"Plans are about all I have," I said, "and they don't amount to much. Just tell him that I'm going out tonight, but I'll be in touch with him the first thing tomorrow."

"I'll tell him, Signor March."

"Thank you—and good night, Signorina Pianta." I put the receiver down and spent a minute feeling sorry for the plain-looking girl, all her glories in the past, waiting around in the hope of sharing what was going on.

I had another drink and then I went in and took a shower. The combination of alcohol and pelting water gave me the illusion of feeling better. But I knew it was just an illusion. A dull anger at what was happening had put a knot in my stomach, and I knew from experience it would stay there until the case was over.

I was working slowly on my fifth drink when the phone rang. I picked it up and answered. It was the desk. They said there was a Signor Marrone to see me. I still didn't know anyone named Marrone, but I told them to send him up. It wouldn't be somebody Johnny Fornessi was sending around this quickly, and it might be somebody with some information to give or peddle.

I slipped on my pants and shirt and waited, working on the drink. Finally there was a knock on the door.

"Avanti," I called.

The door opened and a man came in. He looked almost like a Hollywood version of a comic Italian. He was short and so fat that he looked square. His suit was an expensive one, but it hung on him like a wrinkled tent. His hair was black and curly, although it was beginning to run away from his forehead. His face was swarthy and looked as if it had just been washed in olive oil.

"Signor March?" he asked.

I nodded and indicated the chair. It was the only one in the room, but I was sitting on the bed. He dropped into the chair and mopped his face with a silk handkerchief.

"I am Ugo Marrone," he said, "a journalist."

"Journalist? You mean a reporter?"

"I write a political column," he said, "for *Vie Nuove.*"*

I didn't know the paper. "Very interesting," I said, "but what does it have to do with me? I'm afraid you must have made a mistake."

* An actual weekly publication of the Italian Communist Party; its title translates as "New Ways."

"No mistake," he said. "And it has much to do with you. I wish to talk to you about the death of Anna Maria Pericoloso. I know that you are here to look into her death—or shall we say murder?"

"Does the whole goddam country know my business the minute I land here?" I said. "How do you know that's my reason for being here?"

He smiled and for a minute looked familiar. Or like a bad sketch of somebody I had once known. "I have sources of information within the police," he said. "You were there today seeking information about the girl and shortly afterwards I was told about it."

"And how did you know where to find me?"

"It was nothing," he said, gesturing with his pudgy hands. "I merely called one hotel after another until I found one that had a Signor March registered. You were out at the time, so I took the liberty of coming over later."

"Everybody seems to be taking liberties with me," I said. "All right, what do you want to talk about?"

"Anna Maria Pericoloso. What is your opinion about the case?"

"It is my opinion that the girl is dead," I said and left it like that.

He gave me that same smile again, glancing at me slyly from his fat-framed eyes.

"Do you think she was murdered?" he asked.

"By whom?" I asked innocently.

"By Riccardo Balena or Mario Gambero. Either one or both."

"Who are they?" I asked.

"Do you think that Riccardo Balena's father, who is the Minister of the Interior, ordered the police to cover up for them by calling it an accidental death?"

"Goodness," I said in my most shocked tone. "The police would never do a thing like that, would they? Why, they are the guardians of public safety."

He said a short, hard word. It sounded about the same in Italian as it would have in English. "Signor March," he said, "let us not fence with each other. I know all about the case. I'm sure that you do, too. The girl was murdered and left dead on the beach. Otherwise, where were her clothes? How did she get there at four in the morning? This business of swimming for her health is nonsense. I have spoken to her parents. They are lying. They are frightened."

I shrugged.

"The girl," he continued, "had been running around with young Balena. He had stopped seeing her so often—having found another girl—and she was bothering him. Young Balena is mixed up with Gambero in all sorts of things, including drugs and possibly his Fascist schemes. She was annoying him, and perhaps she knew too much, so they killed her. And then Gambero visited Minister Balena and the police quickly closed the case. It is to your advantage, is it not, to prove that the girl was murdered? The glare of publicity would help you."

"Go ahead and glare," I told him. "I'm not stopping you. If you know so much, you don't need my permission to print it in your newspaper."

"That is true," he admitted. "There are a lot of things we could print. We could just publish the rumors that are all over Rome and demand that Formaggio and Balena resign. But I do not wish to make this so much a political attack."

"What does all that have to do with me?" I asked.

"It is simple. You are now, because of your company, an interested party. So far everyone has insisted that the girl's death was accidental. But if you would state that you are convinced the girl was murdered, I could use that as a point to take off on the rumors and to demand simple justice. It should be most effective."

"I should think so," I said dryly. "And I'd have no trouble winning the contest as the most unpopular man in Italy. Why are you so worried about being accused of political attack? From what I hear, it's going to be political dynamite any way you look at it. What party does your paper represent?"

"Communist."

I stared at him for a minute. "Now I'm beginning to get it," I said. "No, thanks, chum. I have enough trouble pulling my own chestnuts out of the fire without pulling yours, too. I didn't know you Communist writers were able to look so prosperous."

"I am more than just a writer," he said. "I am the political columnist on the paper, but I am also the Chairman of the Central Committee of Rome and I am a member of the City Council."

"You'd better be careful," I told him, "or you'll find yourself accused of fostering the cult of the individual. Or are you up on the latest line?"

"Comrade Togliatti has stated our position very clearly,"* he said stiffly.

"Then get Comrade Togliatti to give you a statement about the girl. Don't bother giving him my regards."

He stood up and stared at me. "You do not like Communists, Signor March? You are an American capitalist tool."

"I'm not much of a tool," I said. "I've had some dealings with Communists—some right here in your country. I remember a time when they were more interested in their own political gains than in fighting the enemy that occupied their country. I don't expect there's been much change."

His face darkened with anger. "And what did you do here in Italy, Signor March? Were not your actions also political? Were you not here for the American capitalists, making sure that the Italian people were sold back into slavery to the same class? I remember your work, Signore."

"Wait a minute," I said. I looked at him more closely. I had the thought a couple of times that there was something familiar about him. Now I looked at him, trying to see him thinner and younger, as he might have been more than a decade earlier. "I've got it," I said. "You were one of the Communists in the underground. We used to call you Ugo, the Ugly One. I remember you now."

"I helped to lead my comrades in the underground," he admitted.

But I was remembering more. "Sure you did," I said. "I remember one night when you were supposed to lead a bunch of your Communists to back up a raid on the Nazis. Only you

* Palmiro Togliatti, leader of the Italian Communist Party.

and your precious group never showed, so the raiding party was hacked to pieces. Only one man escaped, and he died a couple of days later."

"I was doing my duty to the Party and the Italian people "

"Sure. And twenty brave men—part of the Italian people—died because your duty didn't include keeping your word and backing them up. Now get out."

"I—" he began.

"Get out," I said. "Now."

He left. I took another drink to take the taste out of my mouth. It wasn't just him. I was running into too many people who were reminding me of the past—and there wasn't much in it worth remembering.

He'd been there longer than I thought. I'd just finished putting my tie on when there was another knock on the door. I went over and opened it. Piero Roccia, the detective, stood there. He had changed clothes and was looking even more like George Raft. All he needed was to start flipping a coin in the air.*

"Come on in," I said. "I'll be ready as soon as I put my coat on. How goes it?"

"As you'd expect," he said. "There are as yet no leads on the murderer of Attilio. You were right about Johnny Fornessi and Lucky Topo. Both were covered for the time concerned. Johnny Fornessi was with a very important man—a friend of Baron Gambero."

"It figured," I said. I glanced at the bottle and saw there

* In *Scarface,* Raft played a gunman who had a habit of coolly flipping a coin in the air, and it became the trademark gesture of a gangster.

wasn't much left in it. "I was going to offer you a drink, but I guess it'll have to wait until we get to a bar. Anything else?"

"Only this," he said. "I am, as you would say in your country, sticking my neck out. There is no way now to get you a permit to carry a gun. They are very difficult to get under any circumstances. But I have brought you a spare gun of mine. Just be careful who you shoot with it."

"I'm always careful who I shoot," I said. I took the gun and looked at it. I didn't recognize the make, but it looked to be about the same as an American Police .38, only the barrel was shorter. It was loaded.

"And here's a holster for it," he added, dragging it from his pocket. It was a well-worn shoulder holster.

"Piero," I said, "you are an angel in disguise. Is the gun registered to you?"

"As a matter of fact, no," he said. "I have not used this gun for many years and it was never registered. I have taken care of it, however, for it has sentimental value."

I got it. "Resistance days?" I asked.

He nodded. "That gun has shot only Fascists and Nazis. It performed so well that it seemed only right to retire it."

I had strapped the holster under my left arm and slipped the gun into it. I tried it once and it came out easily and with no scraping. "Don't worry, Piero," I said. "If I have to use it, there will be little or no difference between the new targets and the old ones. The worthy gun will not be disgraced."

"It has been a foolish sentiment," he said gruffly.

"Nor will you," I added. "If I am caught with the gun, I will swear that I bought it from Togliatti."

He laughed. "Come. Let us go, Milo."

I buttoned my coat and took a look in the mirror. The gun didn't show. "All ready," I said. "Where are we going?"

"I'm taking you a couple of places," he said as we left the room. "Since I'm sticking my neck out, I might as well stick it out a little farther. First, I will take you to see the girl's parents. I do not think you will get any more out of them than I did—I don't think they even know anything—but you will want to see them."

"Good," I said. "I was going to try to look them up tomorrow. It'll be better with you. Then what?"

"Then we go to dinner. With a young lady."

"You a marriage broker on the side?" I asked.

He shook his head, grinning. "One of the rumors is that young Balena had thrown over Anna Maria for someone else. The only other girl he has been seen with in public is Gianna Bionda, a young movie actress. If she is his new interest, it may be dangerous to fool around with her. But I have arranged for her to have dinner with us."

"You are a man of talent," I said. "I don't know any cops who can produce movie actresses just like that."

"I know her only slightly," he said. He looked embarrassed. "I'm afraid that you are the bait that made her agree to join us."

We were already outside the hotel. Piero had a little Fiat parked there. We got in and he started the motor, pulling into the street.

"I knew that I was a handsome man," I said, "but I didn't know the word had spread so far."

He laughed. "It's not so romantic. Signorina Bionda is a very ambitious girl. She would especially like to go to Hollywood. I merely told her that you were a big American insurance man and pointed out to her that in America many motion pictures are actually financed by insurance companies."

"Not so big," I murmured modestly. "Only a hundred and eighty-five pounds. What am I supposed to do now? Promise to cast her in the next epic I bankroll?"

"That is up to you. I do not think she can give you any actual information, but she is a way to get you into the company of young Balena and Gambero. If young Balena is involved with her, that may make it a little dangerous. He has a reputation for being hotheaded."

"My pal," I said.

"I admit," he said, threading his way through traffic, "that I framed this in my mind without consulting you. It occurred to me that such a situation might be of help. If a man becomes intent on destroying you, he often becomes careless about other things. But I suppose I should have asked you about it."

I looked at him with admiration. "I like it," I said. "It's the kind of thinking I've always used. When you can't get anything on a case, quite often just pushing some of the characters around will do all the work for you. We're going to get along, Piero."

"I thought you would work that way," he said. "It is especially true in a case where there is nothing to get a grip on. If Signorina Bionda tells Gambero and Balena that you are an American insurance man, they will jump to the conclusion that you're here because of Anna Maria. It may make them nervous enough to make mistakes—or to kill you."

"I kill hard," I said.

"I will be limited in the help I can give you during the day," he said, "but when I'm off duty you can depend on me—unofficially."

I nodded. I already knew that without his putting it into words. Just as I knew instinctively that he was a good man to have behind me. I didn't have the slightest idea how we were going to work this one out, but I had every confidence we'd find a way.

We dropped the subject of Anna Maria and talked aimlessly as he drove through Rome. This was my first visit since the war, and we did talk guardedly of the old Rome, but we skirted around the subjects that had involved us both. It was like my conversation with Wilma Pianta. Those were thoughts and deeds which were better forgotten, even if forgetting was impossible. I think that may always be true of war and the deeds connected with it; they are obscenities in the night, not even to be whispered in daylight.

After driving through most of Rome, we finally came to a section of middle-class apartment houses. Piero parked the Fiat in front of one of these and we went in. We walked up to the second floor and he knocked on the door. After a moment it was opened by a woman with a sadly beautiful face, its olive tones framed by pure white hair. She recognized Piero and we walked into the apartment. There was a strong but pleasant smell of garlic in the air.

A masculine counterpart of the woman stood in the living room. His back was bent with age that had been brought on too soon. His face was lined with wrinkles and his hair was as white as the woman's. There were still calluses on the hand that I shook. These were Umberto and Terese Pericoloso, the parents of the girl who had died on the beach.

Piero introduced me and told them I was from the insurance company that had insured their daughter. They exchanged glances.

"We do not care about the money," the father said to me. "We have no one to spend it on."

"I understand," I said. "I am not here because we want to make any trouble about the money. You understand that when we give insurance on a person, that person becomes like a member of our family. We are interested in what happens to him. That is why the company has sent me all the way from America. We would like to know what happened to your daughter." I was cursing myself for putting it that way; but Italian is a language in which you can say it either hard or flowery, and you can't do much in between.

"Anna Maria," said the father, "often did not feel well, and when this happened she would go swimming in the sea during the night. She claimed that this helped her. It was this way the night that she—died." He was picking his way among the words as carefully as if they all had sharp edges.

"Were you both awake when she left?" I asked. They exchanged glances again.

There was no question but that they were frightened. I had a feeling they were afraid of what they didn't know, rather than of some specific thing.

"No," the father said.

"Do you know how she went? Did she drive herself?"

"She didn't have a car," the father said.

"Then how did she go to Ostia?"

"Perhaps a taxi," the father said. You could see that he didn't believe it. "Or perhaps a friend."

"If a friend took her, wouldn't he or she come forward and say so?"

They both shrugged.

"Did she have a date that night?" I asked.

"We don't know," the mother said. "She was out in the evening, but we are not sure where. You understand, Signore, that young girls today are allowed more freedom than when I was a girl. It is said to be the modern way."

"I understand," I told her. "Was your daughter a good swimmer?"

"Oh, yes."

"Don't you think it strange that she should have an accident, then?"

"Perhaps a cramp," the father suggested.

"Did you ever recover her clothes?"

They looked at each other again and I could tell that this was something that bothered them. Then, as though worked by a single string, they both looked at the detective. "Perhaps the police ..." the mother said hesitatingly.

"The police don't have her clothes," I said. "I know how painful all this is to you, but if your daughter's death was not accidental, it's better that those responsible should be punished for it."

They looked frightened again.

"What about boyfriends?" I asked.

"Anna Maria was very popular," the mother answered, glancing at her husband.

"I know that she went out with Riccardo Balena," I said. "Was he her only boyfriend?"

"Oh, no," she said quickly. Too quickly. "She went out with many boys."

"Could you give me the names of the other boys?"

"I—I don't remember," she faltered. "I have forgotten."

"Sure," I said soothingly. "Did she ever have any fights with young Balena?"

"No, no fights," the father said. "If we ever said anything about not wanting her to go out with him, it was only because they came from different positions in life. He is the son of a very fine man. A good man." I noticed that he didn't say that the son had the same qualities as his father.

"Has anyone told you not to say anything, or threatened you in any way?" I asked.

"No," they said together, but it was not very convincing.

"Let me ask you something else," I said. "I know how people feel about this, but would you consent to having an autopsy performed on your daughter?"

"Autopsy?"

"I mean having her examined now to see what caused her death."

"No," he said, almost shouting. "She is to be left alone. Enough has happened to her. Let there be no more. Even the dead have a right to rest."

The mother suddenly started to cry, her face screwed up in a pained mask. The old man put his arms around her, roughly patting her shoulders. His hands had long ago lost their cunning with women, but he was trying.

"Please go," he said over her shoulder. "I do not mean to be unfriendly, but please go. Anna Maria was our only child. There is nothing that can be done that will make her live again. Please leave us with our sorrow." He turned his attention back to his wife, not even waiting to see if we'd leave.

"Let's go," I said to Piero. We turned and walked out of the apartment and down the stairs to the Fiat.

"I'm sorry," I said. "I was trying to go easy on them."

"You were gentle," he said.

"Yeah. It's a nice, lousy business we're in, my friend. We not only nibble on the bones of the dead, we do it in front of the relatives."

He swore as he started the car. "I knew it would be like that, but I thought you should see it for yourself."

"They are certainly frightened. You think they were threatened?"

"Probably. I imagine it was just some vague threat about not involving the boy. In fact, Milo, I do not think they know anything. I think they are frightened of what they do not know."

"Makes sense," I said. "What about at the time? How thorough an examination did the police doctor make?"

"Not much of one. When he examined the body, it was before the whispers had started, and even I still thought it was an accident. By the time I was certain that this was wrong, it was already too late."

"Think we can get an order that will permit an autopsy?"

"Not a chance," he said gloomily. "Not unless things are stirred up a lot more."

"Well, I've got a big spoon," I said. "Where are we picking up this girl?"

"She is a modern woman," he said. "She is meeting us at the restaurant."

"Where?"

"Nino's. On Via Borgognona." He glanced at me and grinned. "I made a reservation in your name. It is not a place where an ordinary detective often goes, but it seemed to me that you should have an expense account."

"I've got one."

"Then we dine on American money," he said. "I wouldn't want you to start out by making a bad impression on the girl. At Nino's you get *bistecca alla fiorentina*—a full kilo of Tuscan beef, the best steak in Italy. And afterwards, May strawberries that are as delicate and sweet-scented as a bride."

"It'll be worth paying for it," I said, "just to finally know a cop who appreciates something more than hamburgers."

"Besides," he continued, "Nino's is a favorite place for writers, artists, journalists, actors—and quite often Baron Gambero and Riccardo Balena."

"Piero, you disappoint me, mixing business with food this way. Well, I suppose we might as well lead the full life. I shall leave my fate in your fine Italian hands."

Another ten minutes of driving brought us to the restaurant. Piero parked the Fiat and we went in. There was something about the immediate atmosphere that reminded me of the European restaurants I'd always liked. This one wasn't gingerbreaded up for the tourists. The walls were bare, as were the tables scattered around the room. A stout lady cashier was perched on a high stool near the door.

"She is here," Piero said. "You see? For an insurance magnate, she is on time."

He led the way across the room. I followed leisurely, examining the girl who waited alone at the table. She was beautiful, of that there was no doubt. She was a blue-eyed Italian blonde, the type you don't see so often in the States. It needed only a glance to show that she was amply provided with the physical traits that are associated with Italian actresses and a few of the more glamorous American stars. In fact, she reminded me more of the American variety. Come to think of it, I mused to myself, this was true of most of the later Italian stars. The American public had originally succumbed to the natural beauty of the Italian stars, but the American attention had made the newer stars succumb to Hollywood standards. They were all becoming as shaved, plucked, and artificial as if they were off the Hollywood assembly line.

"Signorina Bionda," Piero was saying, "may I present Signor March."

"Signor March," she said, making it sound as if it were an impassioned love plea. I couldn't help but wonder how many hours she had practiced doing that with words. But two could play at that game.

"Piero," I said reproachfully, "you did not tell me that I was about to meet the most beautiful woman in the world."

"I wished to have it burst on you unexpectedly," he murmured.

The blonde tried to look modest and only succeeded in giving us a more complete view of her cleavage. It was quite a view. I hated to sit down and lose the advantage of standing above her. I could tell that Piero felt the same way, but we were both gentlemen. We sat down.

"I understand, Signor March, that you are back of many American motion pictures," she said. That girl believed in getting right to the point.

"You might say that," I said, "although I'm not sure how far back."

She laughed as if I were the funniest man in the world. I barely stopped myself from looking around to see if George Gobel* were sitting behind me.

"You look so young to be such a successful man," she said.

"I expect to age rapidly," I told her.

"You are here on business?"

"Yes," I said.

"Then," she said archly, "perhaps I can show you around Rome." It sounded to me as if she were talking more about herself than about Rome.

"I'd like that," I said. I decided I could be as direct as she could. I wanted to use her to get to Baron Gambero, so I might as well jump right in and take the bull by the horns. Or in this case, the cow by the—but I couldn't remember if cows had horns, so I dropped the simile. "As a matter of fact, there are some things I'd like especially to see. Perhaps you can help."

"I'd love to," she said. In her eagerness to please, she leaned

* A popular television comedian of the time.

forward, giving me both barrels of that cleavage again. "What can I do?"

"I'm interested in seeing some of the old estates around Rome," I said. "In fact, I'm told that there's a very interesting old estate south of Rome owned by a ... Baron Gambero, I believe. Perhaps, if I find the exact location, you might go with me one day."

"I can do better than that," she said. "I happen to know Baron Gambero, and I can arrange to take you there." She was still leaning forward, and I was finding it difficult to keep my attention on the conversation.

"Fine," I said.

"Are you looking for locations?" she asked.

"In a way," I said. I made an effort and remembered something else. "By the way, I'd rather that nothing was said about any connections I might have with pictures. You may say that I'm with an insurance company, but that's all."

"I understand," she said. Her tone indicated that we had just entered into a conspiracy to blow up the Vatican.

Piero stepped into the conversation to indicate that a waiter was waiting patiently for us to give him diplomatic recognition. We ordered antipasto for all of us and a bottle of wine. When we'd finished the antipasto, we ordered three steaks.

A slender, nervous little man in a gray suit hurried through the room with a long knife in his hand. Piero must have seen the speculative gleam in my eye, for he told me that this was Nino. The reason for the knife was that he cut all the steaks himself.

Piero had been right about one thing. The steak was charcoal-broiled and one of the best I'd ever had. Each steak must have been more than two pounds and cooked to perfection.

In the meantime, we got the blonde off the subject of me and to talking about herself. She didn't mind at all. We had a rundown on all the parts she'd played, her personal theories about acting, and what she thought about all the other Italian actresses. She kept up a steady flow of talk, meanwhile putting away her two pounds of steak. She chewed and talked, stopping only occasionally to take a deep breath. When that happened, I was never sure which was going to break first—me or the dress.

By the time we'd finished the steak, the blonde and I were Gianna and Milo to each other. Very chummy.

After the steak we had *fragole,* the tiny May strawberries with lemon juice over them, and I'd decided the meal was almost worth a trip to Rome.

Halfway through the strawberries, the blonde let out a squeal. At first I thought the dress had finally given up the struggle, but when I looked I saw she was waving to someone across the room.

"Ricci!" she called.

Two men had entered the restaurant and were headed for a table. One of them was quite young, with a handsome face and close-cropped black hair. He looked as if he were half drunk. The other man was older, probably in his sixties, with a pale, gaunt face. Everything about him was impeccable. The expression on his face gave the impression that he had seen everything in the world and hadn't liked any of it.

I glanced at Piero and he nodded.

The two men were coming over. In a minute they were standing beside our table.

Piero and I stood up.

"May I present Signor March," the blonde said, "and Signor Roccia. Baron Gambero and Signor Balena."

We all said hello politely.

"Signor March is from America," the girl added. She made it sound as if I'd just flown in from Mars. Without a plane.

"That would seem to be obvious," the young man said.

"You must pardon my young friend," the Baron said smoothly. "He is a great admirer of all things American, which means that to balance matters he must be hostile to all Americans."

"That's all right," I said. "We have a lot of people just like him in America. What does the young man do, publish comic magazines?" I knew that there were many Italian businessmen, among the most scornful of American lack of culture, who were busily getting rich on Italian comics, and I was sure they'd know it too.

The Baron laughed and young Balena's face turned a dark red. The poor blonde was in the middle. She didn't want to cut any purse strings. Without thinking, she leaned forward so that all eyes shifted back to her.

"Ricci," she said, "can I see you for just a minute? Alone?"

"All right," he said sulkily.

She got up and looked pleadingly at me. "Excuse me," she said. She moved off to one side with the young man. Piero, the Baron, and I were left standing awkwardly to wait for them.

"He is very young," Baron Gambero said. He managed to suggest a smile without moving the muscles of his face. It was quite a feat. "He still thinks that all women are his own personal domain. It will pass in time."

"It is to be hoped so," I said. I looked at him and pretended to be thinking. "You know, Baron, your name is familiar." I snapped my fingers. "I have it. You and I have a mutual … acquaintance. Johnny Fornessi."

If possible, his face became even more frozen. "Fornessi?" he said. "Oh, yes. An interesting type."

"Quaint," I agreed. If he wanted to play it that way, I was willing to go along. "I knew him in America and you know him in Italy. I guess that gives us a common interest."

Baron Gambero was at least three inches shorter than I, but he managed to give the impression that he was taller. "I suppose it could be so described," he said coldly. "If you gentlemen will excuse me, I will see if our table is ready." He walked stiffly away.

"Well," Piero said dryly, "no one can accuse you of wasting time."

"To hell with it," I said. "If we're going to push, we might as well start right now. As a matter of fact, I think maybe it's better."

He shrugged. "You may be right. We'll probably know when Gianna comes back. By the way, Milo, I'll duck out as soon as we've finished dinner. You want to borrow the Fiat?"

"A borrowed girl, a borrowed gun, a borrowed car," I said. "I ought to have something new and something blue. No, I don't think I'll take the Fiat. It's less work to take taxis. … I've been thinking about something, Piero."

"I'd noticed," he said dryly. "Especially when she leaned over."

"I always think of that," I said. "About the case. All this whispering means that it is teetering on the edge of publicity. What happens when it breaks into the open?"

"All hell breaks loose. The head of our department will undoubtedly have to resign, possibly also the Minister, and it's not impossible that the whole government might fall. Certainly a coalition could bring it about. The Communists and the Socialists are almost strong enough. If one more strong party sided with them "

"This I know," I said impatiently: "I meant what happens with the police. Do they go ahead sitting on the case or do they reopen it?"

He thought about it a minute. "They'd probably reopen it. But that doesn't mean there'd be a lot done."

"What about an autopsy?"

"No chance."

"Think you'd get assigned to it?"

"Probably. Unless I look too eager. But there'd be a limit to what they'd let me do."

"Still, there'd be a lot of advantages to having it out in the open," I said. "For one thing, there'd be less chance of being thrown in the can for stirring around in the case."

"So?" he said. "The point is, my friend, to try to solve the case before it breaks."

"Maybe."

"What are you getting at?"

"Nothing," I said innocently. "I was just thinking out loud.

It's a bad habit I picked up years ago. Forget it. Here comes the blond menace of Rome."

She was coming back across the restaurant with a walk that for the moment threatened the popularity of Nino's food with every male in the place. She was aware of it, too. You could tell by the little smile that played around the corners of her mouth. Although she was pretending to ignore it, she looked about as demure as the star performer in a stag show.

"I am sorry," she said as she reached the table. She sat down, bending forward slowly as though to reward us for having been so patient. "Ricci is a dear, but he can be a bore at times."

"He is in love with you?" I asked.

She shrugged. It was a magnificent shrug, taking in everything from the shoulders to the waist. "He thinks he is," she said, "but he is so young. I prefer more mature men." The glance she sent me from beneath her lashes was meant to convince me of my maturity. "It is all arranged, Milo."

"What is?"

"For us to go to Baron Gambero's place," she said. I didn't miss the slight emphasis on *us*. "He's having a big party this weekend, and you and I are going."

"So you got your boyfriend to agree, but does the Baron know about it?"

"Oh, yes. He made it a definite invitation. The party starts Saturday night."

That would be in two days, I realized. I would have liked to move faster, but I couldn't complain.

"That's fine," I said.

"There's to be a big party Saturday night—and he gives such wonderful parties. Then on Sunday there will be a wild boar hunt—I suppose you'll like that—and Sunday night another party."

"You mean you're allowed to shoot them in Rome?" I asked.

"Who?"

"Bores," I said. "It's very civilized of the Baron." She gave me that George Gobel laugh again. "Oh, you," she said. I think she meant it.

"I hope," I said, "that you didn't tell them that I was a big movie man looking for a location."

"No," she said. "I said that you were an insurance executive. I did tell Ricci that you might be able to help me with my career, but only because he's so jealous. I hope you will forgive me that one little lie." She looked at me with her blue eyes wide and innocent. I decided that her eyes were very effective and that it was probably too bad that most men never got to see them.

We finished our strawberries and had caffè espresso. Piero drank his fast, then glanced at his watch.

"I am very sorry," he said, "but this has been so pleasant and taken so long that I am late for another appointment. Will you both forgive me if I hurry along?" We both assured him that we would. He reminded me to call him the following day and then he left. Gianna and I lingered over our coffee. Finally I called for the bill—it was less than 10,000 lire for the three of us*—and we left. At her suggestion, we stopped

* According to online tables, 10,000 Italian lire would have been about $16 in 1956, and in today's money that would be around $145. The Florentine steak is still on the menu at Ristorante Nino.

in at a couple of nightclubs for drinks. They were both obviously places to see and be seen in. In the second club we ran into an old friend. Johnny Fornessi.

He was at the bar with a girl. A knockout. She had a classic Roman face that was beautiful. Funny how the same sort of face can be beautiful on one girl and not on another. I was thinking of the girl in the Intercontinental office, who had the same kind of face. This girl had deep black hair that fell loosely to her bare shoulders, and she had a figure that made Gianna look underweight. I noticed that even the bartenders didn't pay much attention to what they were mixing. I wondered what she was doing with a guy like Johnny Fornessi.

"Hi, baby," he said to Gianna in English. "You going to be at the party this weekend?"

"Yes," she said. She didn't sound as if she liked him, but that might have been for my benefit. "We have been invited by Baron Gambero."

"So have I, baby," he said with a grin. "Hi, Milo. You seem to be getting around fast."

"It's an old American custom," I said.

"And you've already had an invite from the Baron," he said. He was ignoring the girl with him, not even introducing her, but she didn't seem to mind. "Have you been seeing the sights of Rome?" His grin grew even broader.

"Mostly slum-crawling," I said easily.

"You two know each other?" Gianna said in astonishment.

"Sure," I told her. "Johnny and I knew each other in America. I was walking by a sewer one day when he came crawling out."

"Milo was always a joker," Johnny said, but his grin was getting a little tighter. "I thought you were taking the next plane back to America, Milo."

"Not me," I said lightly. "You know me. I get airsick. I have to stay around Rome for a while just to get up enough nerve to book passage back."

He brayed an artificial laugh. "Milo, you kill me."

"I might at that," I told him. I finished my drink and turned to Gianna. "Do you mind if we go somewhere else? The air in here is a little moth-eaten."

She didn't know what I was talking about, but she was willing to play ball. In fact, she was the most eager ball player I'd ever seen outside of a Yankee training camp. She'd decided I was an integral part of her career and she wasn't going to let go. I had a few twinges of conscience about it as she tagged along when I strode out of the bar.

"Have you ever been to Alfredo's?" she asked when we found ourselves on the street.

"No," I said, "but I'm young yet."

She giggled as I hailed a taxi. We climbed in and she told the driver to take us to Alfredo's.

"You haven't been to Rome until you've been to Alfredo's," she said. For some reason, she sounded like a tourist. "There are three Alfredo's in Rome, but we are going to the original one. In the Piazza Augusto Imperatore. We should be just in time for the late dinner crowd and we can see Alfredo himself."

"I can hardly wait," I said. She thought this was funny, too. She was determined to be the best audience I ever had.

The taxi finally pulled to the curb. We went into the restaurant. I might as well have been back in New York. I was willing to bet that two-thirds of the people there were tourists, some of them well-known ones. The walls of the restaurant were covered with photographs of celebrities. The hat check girl looked as if she'd just come in off Broadway.

At Gianna's insistence we got a table instead of going into the bar. We ordered some odds and ends to chew on, plus more coffee and brandy. Then I excused myself. I'd made up my mind about something. I was going to take a flyer on a long shot. I knew it was going to be like turning loose an avalanche, not knowing which way it was going to go. But if this case was going to be solved by pushing, I might as well start pushing everybody in sight.

I found a public phone and a Rome directory. I looked up Ugo Marrone's phone number and called him.

"Pronto," a voice finally said. I recognized his voice. He sounded sleepy.

"Questo è Milo March," I said.

"Yes?" He didn't sound sleepy any longer.

"I've been thinking about it," I said, "and I've decided to give you what you want. Or at least part of it."

"Why?" he asked.

"I'm soft-hearted," I said. "I've been sitting here feeling sorry for the poor, downtrodden Italian Communist leaders, forced to wear silk suits whether they want to or not. My new slogan is: 'Workers of the world, unite—you have nothing to lose but your denims.' "

He called me a name that was no compliment to my mother.

"Careful, Ugo, old comrade. I bruise easily, and don't forget that I come bearing gifts."

He was silent for a minute and I could picture him mopping his face with that silk handkerchief. "What will you give us?" he asked finally.

"You may quote me," I said, "as a representative of the Intercontinental Insurance Company, as saying that I am convinced that Anna Maria Pericoloso was murdered. End of quote. If you say one more thing about me, or even imply that I said anything beyond that, I'll sue you for every lira of your Moscow gold. Not to mention the few things which I will do to you personally."

"Are you threatening me?"

"Yes," I said cheerfully.

"Why do you suddenly want us to publish this?" he asked. "What kind of trick are you planning?"

"You wound me, Comrade Ugo," I said. "Deeply. My ulterior motives are the same as your own. I want to see the case brought out into the open. I deplore whispering—except in the bedroom. Let the clear light of truth shine on everything."

"You know," he asked suspiciously, "what we expect to accomplish with this murder?"

"Sure. You think it will cause the overthrow of the present government and that you can tie it to so many men that you will be able to take over."

"You are a tool of American capitalists," he said. "Why are you willing to let this happen?"

I grinned at the phone. "I didn't say that I was willing to let it happen. I'm merely willing to let you try. In fact, I couldn't stop you if I wanted to. Sooner or later, you're going to print the story anyway. I'm just letting you pretend that I brought it up instead of politics."

"It's true you couldn't stop us," he said thoughtfully. "I just don't understand what you expect to get out of it. A man like you does nothing without a reason."

"I think it will help me to catch a murderer," I said honestly.

"Perhaps. And when you catch your murderer, he will be revealed as Riccardo Balena. Which is good. I will even help you catch your murderer."

"You," I said, "couldn't even catch a cold unless B and K cabled you instructions.* Good night, Comrade Ugo." I hung up without waiting for his reply and went back to the blonde.

It seemed I was just in time. She told me excitedly that she'd been afraid I was going to miss the real reason for coming to Alfredo's.

"A fan dance by Marilyn Monroe?" I guessed.

"Silly," she said. "Somebody just ordered *Maestosissime Fettuccine all'Alfredo.*"

"Somebody ordered a dish of buttered egg noodles?" I said. "That's going to cause a sensation? And I thought Rome was a lively town."

"You'll see," she said. "It's starting now."

The lights in the restaurant were dimmed and a spotlight was suddenly thrown on one table. There was a roll of drums and a short, red-faced man with a prominent mustache bounded into the light. Waiters appeared with plates, bowl,

* "B and K" are likely Bulganin and Khrushchev, heads of the Russian government at the time.

and forks and spoons. The little man started tossing noodles around, banging on the plate and shouting loudly, like a juggler auditioning for *The Ed Sullivan Show.* Several times it looked as if the noodles would win the bout, but he finally had them all pinned in a neat pile on the plate. The waiters started to applaud and the customers joined in. The little man blew kisses in every direction and departed.

"He's been doing that for years," she said. "People come for miles to see him mix noodles. Why, do you know that Mary Pickford and Douglas Fairbanks once gave him a gold spoon and fork to mix with?"

"I'm speechless," I said with a rare amount of honesty. "I am forever in your debt, Gianna. If I had missed this, I'm sure that I would never have forgiven myself. And what would I have told my grandchildren when they wanted to know what I did in Rome?"

She giggled again.

Just out of curiosity I looked at the menu. *Maestosissime Fettuccine all'Alfredo* cost 260 lire. That was a hell of a lot of work for forty cents.

We left Alfredo's and started covering the Roman night-clubs. Gianna was demonstrating that she was a two-fisted drinker. The only visible effect of her drinking was that as the evening wore on it seemed that she revealed more and more cleavage when she leaned forward. I decided that there must be some sort of Gresham's Law that controlled such matters.

Once we ran into Johnny Fornessi and his good-looking girl, but we didn't stop for any light conversation. Twice, also, we encountered Baron Gambero and young Balena. Each time, the young man glared and the Baron bowed formally. We met a number of other men and women Gianna knew, apparently part of a group that spent every night this way. I wondered, as I often had in nightclubs, if they didn't get tired of seeing each other night after night. I had seen most of them only once, and I was pretty tired of them already.

Finally at about two in the morning we gave up. It was just as well. Not only was I tired, but if this kept up, Intercontinental's expense money would get pretty limp. We took a taxi to Gianna's apartment house.

"I have some wonderful brandy that Baron Gambero gave me," she said. "Would you like to come up for a drink?" There didn't seem to be much doubt that she also had etchings.

"I think I'll take a rain check," I said lightly. "It's been a long, hard day."

She pouted. "I've been saving it for a special occasion," she said.

I was going to feel pretty silly fighting for my honor in an Italian taxi, but I felt more like doing that than going up to her apartment. I'd listened to her chattering so damn much, I couldn't think of her in any other role.

"Let it get a day or two older," I suggested. "Brandy is always better when it's older. I'll call you tomorrow."

"All right," she said reluctantly. "And don't forget our party this weekend."

"As if I could ever," I said. Saying good night took another two minutes, but she finally got out of the cab and went into the building. I told the driver to take me to the Bernini Hotel.

I was really ready to hit the sack when I reached the hotel. I went straight up to my room. I unlocked the door and stepped inside. Then I stopped. Something sharp was pressing against my throat.

"Calma," a voice said softly. "My knife is sharp."

FOUR

There's something about the sharp edge of a knife that makes a man stand still when he's told to. You don't argue. At the same time, if a knife is touched to your throat in the dark and a voice tells you to take it easy, there's hope. If he just wanted to kill you, you'd already be dead.

"Che succede?" I asked.

"Who killed my brother?" the voice asked. "You, Signore?"

"I haven't killed anybody recently," I said, "and I'm not even sure that I know anybody's brother. If you want to talk about it, how about taking the knife away? My throat works better without a knife hugging it."

He didn't make any move to take it away. "You were there, Signore. I saw you."

"I've been lots of places today," I said. "Turn on the light and we'll talk about it."

"No," he said. "Why were you there, Signore?"

My eyes had adjusted to the darkness and I could see his outlines. He didn't look very big. He was standing in front of me and a little to the right.

I didn't think he was intending to kill me, but I was tired of that knife at my throat. He might be nervous and push a little harder than he meant to. The only answer was to do something about it.

There wasn't much room behind me, but I thought it was enough. I took a quick step backward, bringing my right hand up to grasp his wrist. Because of the darkness, he almost eeled out of my grasp, but I clamped my fingers down and held on. Then I gave it a sharp twist. He cursed as the knife thudded on the carpet.

Still holding him, I reached around with my other hand and found the light switch. I flicked it on. Twisting his arm, I threw him from me. I bent down and picked up the knife. It had a long, thin blade and I could see it was razor sharp. A nasty little toy.

Then, finally, I looked at him. And was surprised. He was only a boy. In size, he looked no more than twelve, but there was an old look about his face, so I guessed he was more than that. He was staring at me with sullen hatred.

"Now, what's this all about?" I asked.

"I will kill you," he said. It was almost a whisper.

"Look," I said patiently. "I haven't killed anyone. I don't know you and I don't know your brother. Now, sit down on the bed and tell me what the hell you're talking about." I hefted the knife a minute and then tossed it to him.

He caught it, looked at me uncertainly, and finally put it away among his ragged clothing.

"How old are you?" I asked.

"I am a man," he said defiantly.

"I didn't say you weren't a man. I asked how old you are."

"Sixteen."

I nodded to myself. That explained the oldness of his face. He'd been about five years old while Italy was occupied. I remembered kids like him. In those days so many of them either starved to death or got out and hustled—their sister, somebody else's sisters, black market goods, anything that would make a lira. They'd learned a lot about life in a very short time and none of them had ever had a childhood.

"What's your name?" I asked.

"Achille Coniglio."

There was something familiar about the name and then I remembered what it was. That had been the last name of the informer Piero had sent me to see. And he'd been killed.

"Attilio was your brother?" I asked.

He nodded.

"I did not kill your brother," I told him. I hesitated, wondering if he knew what his brother did. Then I decided that he must. There were no secrets from the kids who had grown up in the streets. "You know that your brother sometimes gave information to a detective at the police station?"

"Sold it," he said proudly. "My brother was very smart. He knew everything that was going on in Rome and he made a good thing of it."

"Yeah. Well, the detective had told me to go see your brother at the Martello and he could tell me something that I wanted to know rather badly. I was delayed in getting there, and when I arrived the police told me that your brother had been killed. That is all I know about it, Achille."

He studied me for a minute, then stood up from the bed. "I am sorry that I have bothered you, Signore." He started for the door.

"Where are you going?" I asked.

He shrugged. "I will find the killer of my brother."

"Sit down, Achille," I said. "Perhaps you and I can work together, man to man, to find the killer of your brother. I would also like to find him."

He went back to the bed and sat down, watching me. He wasn't unfriendly. Neither was he friendly. He was a businessman waiting to hear another businessman's proposition.

"What about your mother and father?" I asked.

"They are dead, Signore. They were both killed during the war."

"Your brother raised you?"

He nodded.

"Any other brothers or sisters?"

He hesitated. "We had a sister. She died maybe a year after the war. She had baby and they both died. She was only thirteen." He added the last as though he meant it to be an apology.

"I understand about those matters," I told him. "I was in Rome during the bad days."

"You came with the soldiers?"

"No, I was here before. Many months before."

"Then you were with the underground?"

"Yes."

"Perhaps you knew my father," he said eagerly. "My father fought with the underground and it was thus that he was killed."

"Perhaps," I said gently. "I knew many who were with the underground, but usually we knew each other only by first names or by special names. Tell me, Achille, how did you get into my room?"

"With this," he said. He proudly produced a strip of steel.

"You are a talented man," I said solemnly. "Do you know my name?"

"Si, signore. It is Milo March."

"Since we are to be friends and brothers in a cause, you may call me Milo. Just as I will call you Achille."

He nodded.

"Do you know why I am here, Achille?"

"No ... Milo. I know only that you are a rich American."

"Not a rich American," I said, even though I knew he wouldn't believe me and that there was no way of explaining it to him. By his standards, I was rich. "Do you know the name of Anna Maria Pericoloso?"

He wrinkled his forehead. "The girl who was found dead on the beach?"

"Yes," I said. "She was murdered. I am here to find out who killed her. The same person—or someone helping him—killed your brother. I was trying to see your brother because I thought he might have some information I needed. Somebody else thought he did, too. Perhaps you can also help with information at times. And I will pay you as I would have paid your brother."

"I will do my best, *signo*—Milo," he said.

"In the meantime, where can I find you if I want you?"

"I live above the wineshop on Via Rana. If I am not there, you can always leave a message for me in the wineshop."

"I will do it," I said. "In the meantime, you might listen for anything concerning the girl on the beach. And I will be remembering your brother. Since it is to be a business proposition, I will give you this in advance." I took out a 5,000 lire note and handed it to him. "Shall we shake hands on it?"

We shook hands gravely.

"I will work very hard," he said. "I will do work that would have made my brother proud."

"I'm sure you will, Achille," I said. "But now it is very late. We will be in touch with each other. Good night."

"Good night," he said. He stood up and we shook hands again. Then he left. It was three o'clock in the morning. I didn't waste any more time even thinking about the case. I just went to bed.

It was about ten o'clock when I awakened the next morning. I phoned downstairs and asked them to send up some breakfast. I went in and had a fast shower while they were sending it. I came out and slipped into slacks and a shirt. By that time, my breakfast was there.

I had just finished eating when there was a knock on the door. I thought it was the waiter back for the dishes. *"Avanti,"* I called.

The door opened and a man stepped inside. I'd never seen him before, but he had an official look about him. Not like a cop. Something bigger. It was partly the clothes and partly the way he wore them. He might have been any nationality; he would have looked the same in any country.

"Mr. March?" he asked. He was using English.

"Who let you in?" I demanded.

"You just did," he said. There was a lot of frost on his smile. "You told me to enter."

"I'll have to watch that carelessness," I said. "What do you want?"

"I'm Albert Blaine from the American Embassy."

"Sorry," I told him. "I don't want to buy any ambassadors today."

The frost got a little thicker. "Mr. March," he said, "have you seen the morning papers?"

"No. Why should I? The Italian papers don't carry *Peanuts.*"

"Specifically, have you seen this paper?" He produced one from behind his back. By squinting I could see that it was *Vie Nuove.*

"No," I said. "Should I?"

"You most certainly should have," he said grimly. "Permit me, Mr. March, to read to you what it says." He unfolded the paper crisply and read: "Mr. Milo March, representative of the American firm of Intercontinental Insurance, in an exclusive interview, stated that he was convinced that Anna Maria Pericoloso was murdered."

"Sounds all right," I said mildly. "I'm Milo March. I am a representative of Intercontinental Insurance. They are an American company. I suppose it was an exclusive interview; nobody else was present. Anna Maria Pericoloso was murdered. Everything seems to be in order."

He was breathing hard, but in a genteel fashion. "Mr. March, are you aware what newspaper this is?"

"Italian?" I guessed brightly.

I was aware that beneath the jacket of his Saville Row suit Mr. Blaine's heart was beating rapidly, but he was determined that Groton and Harvard would carry the day. I had to admire his restraint.

"Mr. March," he said slowly, *"Vie Nuove* is the largest

Communist newspaper in Italy, a country which has two million registered Communists."

I opened my eyes as wide as I could. "Communist?" I said. "He never told me that. He merely said he was a journalist. That was very unfair of him, wasn't it?"

I'm sure that Mr. Blaine loved his job, but at that moment he would have probably traded it in to become a deck hand on a cattle boat.

"Not only is it a Communist paper," he said, "but you couldn't have found a more explosive subject if you tried. *Vie Nuove* uses your statement to imply that the murder of the girl was committed by Riccardo Balena, whose father is the Minister of the Interior and an integral factor of the Christian-Democrat government. They do it so successfully that a few independent papers are already out demanding that Balena resign. By the weekend, they may very well be demanding that the entire government resign. The Communists will certainly be doing so. They may even succeed and be able to use this to get in power. If the Communists capture the government, they will have you, Mr. March, to thank for it."

"You flatter me," I muttered modestly.

He took a deep breath. "Not only that, Mr. March, but the news of your little interview has already been cabled to papers back in the States. I am afraid we'll be hearing about this from the State Department. I have no doubt there will be other calls throughout the day."

"Seems like a lot of fuss to make over one little accident."

"Little accident!" he said. Groton and Harvard almost lost the battle.

"Mr. March, we know all about you. You are a trouble-maker. At least twice before you have almost caused an international incident."

"Once for the State Department and once for Central Intelligence," I said.

"That is beside the point. I'm aware that you have served your country. But you seem oblivious to the fact that actions have consequences. Sometimes very serious ones. You will do anything that helps your immediate task."

I gave him my most angelic smile.

"I have a suggestion for you, Mr. March."

"Don't say it," I said in mock horror. "It's very unseemly for diplomats to use the kind of language you're thinking."

"Mr. March," he said grimly, "there is a plane leaving Rome for New York in two hours. I suggest that you be on it."

"Oh, I couldn't do that. I have a date for the weekend, and it might cause a lot of bad feeling if I didn't show up. Don't forget, Mr. Blaine, that every American in Europe is a sort of unofficial ambassador."

"You are aware that we can send you back?"

"I'm aware that you can try," I said. I decided it was time to stop playing around. "I also think it might make quite a stink, Mr. Blaine. Intercontinental is an American company, but it is also an Italian company. I work for them and am entirely within the scope of my job when I say that I am convinced one our policyholders was murdered. That is not interfering with the Italian government. Even if the murderer should be a member of the government and I catch him, I'm not playing politics. But you are. True, you want to help keep the present government in power, but anything you do to that end is interfering in the internal affairs of Italy. All you have to do is toss me out of here and every newspaper in Europe will be on your neck. And think what the Communists will do with it."

He knew that was true but he wasn't going to admit it. "I didn't say we were sending you back," he said stiffly. "I merely said that we can. If necessary, we will."

"Relax, buster," I said. "There isn't even a bootblack in Rome who wasn't already convinced that young Balena murdered this girl. Even if he's guilty, it's better to find out and get it over with. Maybe he isn't guilty. Either way it's better to get it out of the rumor gutters. I've got a hunch it'll all be wrapped up by the first of next week."

"I hope, for your sake, you're right. In the meantime, don't give out any more interviews without checking with us first. And stay where we can find you."

"That'll be easy. I'm invited to spend the weekend at the estate of Baron Gambero. Maybe you can bribe one of the servants to send you hourly reports."

"As a matter of fact, I am going to be there myself," he said. He didn't sound too happy about it. "I shall make it a point of watching you, Mr. March."

"Even in the bedroom?" I asked. "There's a blonde ..." His eyebrows expressed his opinion of me.

"On your way out," I said, "close the door."

He did. But not gently.

He was barely out of the room when my phone rang. I picked up the receiver and said hello. It was Luigi Manzo. He was pretty excited.

"Have you seen the morning newspapers?" he asked.

"No," I said, "but I've heard about it. A member of the American Embassy was just here."

"We'll sue them!"

"Who? The Embassy?"

"Vie Nuove. We'll get the best lawyer in Rome. I know just the man and—"

"Calma," I told him. "I authorized them to say that I was sure Anna Maria Pericoloso was murdered, if that's what you're talking about."

"But—but why?"

"Look, Luigi," I said, "I can't spend the next six months going around Rome giving an imitation of Sherlock Holmes. This way, the murderer knows that I'm after him. It should frighten him and maybe he'll make a mistake, maybe even try to kill me. But if he's scared, then I'm that much closer to him."

"But why *Vie Nuove?* Why not *Il Mondo* or some other paper?"

"It'll make a bigger stink this way," I said. "If you raise a big enough stink, people will throw open a lot of windows. That's what we want—all the windows open and a lot of fresh air blowing in."

"I guess you know what you're doing," he said. "I surely hope it turns out that way. I have been afraid that Intercontinental might become discouraged and decide to close the Rome office."

"Because of one case?" I said. "Don't be foolish."

"Not just this one case, no," he said. "It's this case on top of all the losses."

"What losses?"

"We've only been open here two years," he said. "We've sold a lot of policies, but we've also had to pay off on an unusual number of them. It has been a streak of bad luck."

"In two years?" I exclaimed. "How many policies?"

"I don't remember the exact number offhand, but it's about twenty percent of the number we've sold."

I whistled softly to myself. With the office open only two years, they shouldn't have had to pay off on any policies yet.

"What did the New York office say about it?" I asked him.

"Agreed it was bad luck and raised the rates on older people. A number of those involved were elderly, although the doctor had said they were in good health."

"How did they die?"

"Oh, natural deaths. A few accidents maybe."

"Do me a favor, Luigi," I said. "I wanted you to send over the Pericoloso file. Now, if it's not too much trouble, I'd like the pertinent facts on all the cases that have been paid off. I don't mean names or anything like that. But see if you can get the girl to run through the files and dig up the number of cases, how they died, and how much money was involved."

"You think something is wrong?" he asked. He sounded worried.

"Just say I'm curious," I told him. "You'll send them over to the hotel?"

"As soon as I can," he said. We said good-bye and hung up.

It was going to be a busy day. In the next fifteen minutes I had four phone calls. All of them were from newspaper reporters wanting an interview. I said "No comment" so often

I began to sound like a presidential assistant. Then there was a knock on the door and it was a boy with a cable.

It was from Martin Raymond, the Intercontinental vice-president in New York. It read:

WHAT'S THIS ABOUT COMMUNIST TIE-IN? HAVE YOU FLIPPED?
RAYMOND

I grinned, then phoned downstairs and dictated a cable to be sent to him. Mine read:

I THOUGHT THE MAN WAS FROM MOSCOW, IDAHO. CAN'T YOU SMELL AN INSURANCE RING WHEN IT'S RIGHT UNDER YOUR NOSE?
LOVE, MILO

I sent it collect.

The next phone call was one I was more interested in. It was Piero.

"I'm calling from outside," he said. "My friend, you certainly stirred up a hornet's nest."

"I know," I said. "The hornets have been buzzing."

"Not all of them. There was a high-level meeting at the national police headquarters this morning devoted entirely to you. There was even a member of your Embassy there."

"Blaine?"

"I think that was his name."

"He came around to see me afterwards. He didn't mention the police, but he was all set to boot me out of the country."

"What happened?"

"I refused to bend over."

He sighed heavily. "I hope you know what you are doing, Milo, my friend."

"I know," I said. I told him the same thing I'd told Luigi, only in a little more detail.

"I think you're right," he said reluctantly, "but it is dangerous. In the meantime, you're right on at least one point. The case of Anna Maria Pericoloso has been reopened."

"Who's assigned to it?"

"I am," he said glumly.

"You don't sound very happy about it."

"Why should I be? I am being set up as the first sacrificial goat. I am under orders to ask no questions of either Baron Gambero or Riccardo Balena, nor to ask any questions about them."

"All right, I'll ask them," I said. "Gianna and I ran into the Baron a couple of times last night and he bowed to me twice. I figure that makes me practically a count. What are you supposed to do?"

"They didn't say."

"Okay," I said. "I can tell you the first thing to do. Demand an autopsy."

"We won't get it."

"Demand it anyway," I said. "If you can, call me again after you've asked for that."

"All right," he said. "I'll call you from outside. Don't try to reach me at headquarters. If they know we're friendly, they'll probably take me right off the case."

"Okay," I said. "I'll wait to hear from you."

We hung up. After that my phone was idle for a couple of minutes, so I took advantage of it to call downstairs and order a new bottle of brandy and some ice. When the waiter delivered it, I took a good healthy drink. I had a feeling I was going to need it.

I had a couple of more calls from newspapers; there was one call from an indignant American tourist who'd seen the newspaper. He wanted to know what kind of a louse I was.

"The ordinary genus *Pediculus* kind," I told him, and he hung up in indignation.

After that things calmed down a little. I stretched across the bed and drank brandy and thought about the case. I still didn't have much to go on, but I had a feeling that the pushing was going to produce results.

There was a knock on the door.

"Avanti," I called, before it occurred to me that it might be another unwelcome visitor.

The door opened and Wilma Pianta came hesitatingly into the room. She looked just as mousy and middle-aged as she had in the office. She had a big folder under her arm.

"Signor Manzo asked me to bring you these papers," she said.

"I know," I said. "Thank you, Signorina Pianta. Won't you sit down for a minute? I'm sorry my quarters aren't more comfortable."

"Prego," she said. She handed me the papers and sat down, perching on the edge of the chair as though she were poised for flight. Her eyes flickered past the bottle of brandy and the glass beside me.

"Would you like a drink of brandy?" I couldn't think of anything else to offer her, but I wouldn't have been surprised if she had taken off like a startled bunny.

"That might be nice," she said.

I was so surprised that it took me a minute to get to my feet. "I can give it to you with water, just with ice, or straight," I said.

"With ice, I think," she said.

I got another glass from the bathroom, dropped some ice in it, and splashed in brandy. I handed it to her.

"Grazie," she said.

I replenished my own glass. *"Vuoi una sigaretta?"* I asked.

"Permesso."

I gave her a cigarette and lit it.

"Grazie," she said again. We were getting as formal as hell.

I lit a cigarette for myself. Then I lifted my glass. *"Alla sua salute,"* I said.

"Salute," she responded gravely.

She drank and then suddenly smiled. It made her look younger and more attractive. "It is like the old days," she said. "We would often have brandy to keep us warm just before a raid."

"I remember," I said. "Only it was usually *grappa.*"

"From the nearest farmhouse," she added.

We both laughed, yet there was no humor in our laughter. There was only a vaguely shy memory, filled with many things. There is something about going through guerrilla warfare that is impossible to describe. It's quite different from anything else in war or peace. It's a world in which all life, including your own, is cheap. You exist minute by minute and by virtue of your own wits. You have close relationships, but they're not like any others; each of you is aware that the other may be dead tomorrow, so you don't get too close. When it's over, you want to forget it, but you can't. You wouldn't go back to it for anything in the world, but everything you ever do again is stale and flat. You remember it with horror and sympathy and longing. You wake up in the middle of the night, bathed in a cold sweat, remembering the feel of a knife against your throat; in the middle of the day, while going over your budget and wondering where to get the extra ten bucks for the electric bill, you will suddenly remember what it was like to steal through a frost-cloaked night with a knife in your hand. When you meet someone else who has shared your experience—as Wilma Pianta and I had met—each of you will be afraid of the other, but you will also have a bond you can never have with anyone else.

"To the old days," I said.

"The old days," she repeated.

We both drank again. That was the end of two drinks. Without asking, I took her glass and fixed two more. I gave her glass to her again.

"It's odd that we never met," I said. "I remember hearing of La Ragazza from the day I first parachuted into Italy. Once, I remember, we raided the same Nazi post. Your group hit them one night and mine did the next night."

"I remember The American, too," she said. "There were many Americans here then, but did you know that you were called 'The American'? I even saw you once. In the Piazza

Venezia when Mussolini was making a speech. You were pointed out to me by the man who was with me. He told me that you had already killed twenty Nazi officers. I was very jealous because that was two more than I had killed."

I could understand that, too. "He was probably exaggerating," I said. "They did that a lot in those days, too."

"I know," she said.

While she had been talking, her hand had been stroking the worn leather of the shoulder holster I'd borrowed from Piero. It was hanging over the back of the chair on which she sat. Suddenly she seemed to become aware of it.

"I see," she said, "that your life does not seem to have changed so much since the old days."

"More than it appears," I said.

Her hand brushed the grip of the gun in the holster and I could see her fingers trembling. "I never liked guns," she said.

The whole scene was beginning to get me. I looked at her, middle-aged and plain, and I could imagine her standing in front of her mirror for hours thinking of what it had once been like. She'd been the girl of the underground, feared by the Fascists and Nazis and revered by everyone else, and now her hands touched nothing more dangerous than a typewriter.

I stood up, wanting to make some gesture toward her, to reassure her that she was still an individual of importance. I'm not sure what I wanted to do, but I think it was something as simple as a pat on the head—the way you will absent-mindedly pat a child on the head to reassure him. But it didn't turn out that way.

I stretched my hand out toward her. Then, suddenly, she

was on her feet, the glass of brandy splashing to the carpet, and into my arms. Her lips met mine with a fierce impact. Something lighted a fire between us.

There were no words. Our lips parted reluctantly and we moved apart with the precision of dancers, our hands going to catches, buttons, and zippers. I felt like a sleepwalker as I removed my clothing.

I turned to look at her and got my second shock. Gone was the middle-aged, plain-looking woman; in her place stood a beautiful young woman, her olive skin flushed. Her black hair was down around her shoulders. She'd taken off her glasses and her face was warmly alive. Her body, tinted pink and ivory, was one of the most beautiful I'd ever seen. I touched her and then she was all fire and wildness.

Later, I lit two cigarettes and passed one of them to her. It seemed like another age when we had last spoken to each other.

"Why the disguise?" I asked.

I could feel her shrug. "When it's there, it's no disguise," she said. Her voice sounded distant and drained.

I glanced at her, expecting to see that her beauty had fled, but it was still there. Her face, framed by the wild black hair, was soft and relaxed. There was something familiar about it, as though I had seen it years before. Maybe, in a way I had.

She snubbed out the cigarette and stood up. I watched her as she dressed, as the beauty vanished layer by layer beneath the shapeless clothes. She pulled back her hair and put on the glasses. The middle-aged, plain woman had returned and the spell was over.

She stared at me for a moment, then turned and walked from the room. That, too, was like the old days. Then people had mated swiftly and passionately, and afterwards there had been no tenderness; one was careful not to build up something which death might take the next minute.

I went in and had a shower. When I came back, I picked up her glass and put it in the bathroom. I took a towel and rubbed at the wet stain of brandy. When that was done, there was no trace of her; she might never have been there.

I poured myself a drink and stretched out on the bed with the folder. I opened it and started reading.

There was nothing important that I didn't already know in the file on Anna Maria Pericoloso. There were a lot of details about her height and weight and health, but with the girl in the cemetery they were nothing but statistics. 0.001585

The rest of the folder was the information I wanted. It was simple and to the point. In the two years that Intercontinental had been operating as an Italian company, it had sold 1,012 policies. In that period 193 policyholders had died. Fourteen listed as accidental deaths—car accidents, drownings, and one fall from a building—and the rest as natural deaths. They had run in age from 53 to 65. All supposedly had been in good health at the time of taking their policies. The total amount paid to beneficiaries was 95,550,000 lire, or about $150,000.* A nice hunk of change to lose in two years.

I thought about it for a while. There wasn't anything to pin down, but I was sure my first hunch was right. I picked up the phone and called the office.

* About $1.4 million in today's money.

Luigi Manzo answered the phone. "Milo," he said, "I've been waiting to hear from you. I've been worried about those policies that have been collected. Do you think there is something wrong?"

"Do you?" I countered.

"I didn't," he said. "I knew the percentage was high, but I confess you have me worried. I've put a lot into this and have had big plans about it."

"Don't worry," I said. "Even if something is wrong, the company can't blame you unless they give you the setup to investigate every case. Now, I want you to do something else for me."

"Anything," he said fervently. "But how could anything be wrong? The doctors—"

"Doctors are just as venal as the rest of us," I said. "Look in your files while I hold on and pull out the folder on the latest policy to be paid."

"You mean before Pericoloso?"

"Yes. Her policy hasn't been paid yet."

"Just a minute," he said.

I held the receiver and waited. It was almost three minutes before he was back.

"Sorry it took so long," he said. "Signorina Pianta is not yet back and I am not familiar with the filing system. But I have it now. The last insured one to die was a man named Giulio Ferrara."

"In Rome?" I asked.

He gave me the address where the man had lived. "When?" I asked.

"A month ago."

"Cause of death?"

"Heart failure."

"Every death is a heart failure," I said, groaning. "All right. Who was the beneficiary?"

"Rossana Caradonna. A niece."

"Same address?"

"No." It took him a minute to find it, but then he gave it to me.

"How long was the policy in force?"

"One year and three months."

"Amount?"

"Six hundred and fifty thousand lire."

"All right, Luigi," I said. "I probably won't talk to you again until the first of the week. Maybe by then we'll have everything wrapped up. Maybe."

"Would you like my home number if you should want me?"

"I don't think I'll need it, but give it to me anyway."

"Roma 64397."

I wrote it down. "I'm going to Baron Gambero's estate tomorrow," I said, "and won't be back until Sunday night. But I'll call you the first thing Monday morning. Have a nice weekend."

"I'll try," he said gloomily. *"Buona fortuna,* Milo."

"Grazie," I said. I hung up.

I became aware that it was late and I hadn't had any lunch. I phoned downstairs and had them send something up to me. I had another drink to give me an appetite. The phone rang.

It was Piero. "No," he said when I answered.

"No what?"

"No autopsy."

"So we expected that," I said. "Now we know. Did they give any reasons?"

"A thousand," he said. "The girl's parents object. The church would object. Public opinion would object. It would help the political opposition because they would want to know why we didn't do it before. It would look as if the Communists had only to crack the whip to make us jump. And so on. And you still have no chance of winning a popularity contest in the Ministry of the Interior."

"Someday," I said, "I'm going to go on one of those television quiz programs and pick the category of people who don't like me."

"Shall I phone *Lascia o Raddoppia** and tip them off about you?" he asked. "You can win as much as a half million lire."

"You mean you've got them here, too?" I groaned. "There's no place left to hide. ... What are you doing, Piero?"

"Running between a public phone and headquarters," he said bitterly. "What else? And if they knew that I—first-class detective Piero Roccia—had become merely an errand boy for an American insurance detective, you know what would happen?"

"Sure," I said. "They'd put you back into uniform and transfer you to a beat on Sullivan Street in New York.** But what are you really doing with your time?"

"Trying to look busy. Why?"

---

* "Leave It or Double It," an Italian quiz show similar to *The $64,000 Question*.

** In the heart of Manhattan's Little Italy.

"A couple of things, Piero. You talked to the Pericoloso family more than I did. Do you think they might have agreed to split the insurance money with anyone?"

He thought a minute. "No. Why?"

"Just an idea. If you get a chance, try to get in touch with them and see if anyone approached them, wanting a cut of the money. I don't think you'll uncover anything, but we might as well make certain."

"All right. What else?"

"I want you to find out everything you can about two people. Giulio Ferrara and Rossana Caradonna." I gave him the addresses. "Giulio is dead. He died about a month ago. Rossana is his niece. See what you can dig up about their relationship. Did they get along, stuff like that. You know what to look for as well as I do."

"Why are you interested in them?" he asked.

"I don't think it has anything to do with the Pericoloso girl," I said, "although it might. But there have been an unusual number of insured persons dying in Rome in the past two years. I'm curious about it, even if it doesn't tie in. Call it an occupational disease. Do you mind?"

"Why should I? I've got to do something or I will go out of my mind sitting around and thinking about the things I can't do. I suppose you want all the information sometime yesterday?"

"That's the general idea," I said. "I'm going out pretty soon. If I'm not in when you call, keep calling back every half hour or so. I may have another idea for us tonight."

"Imagine what *Vie Nuove* would do with it," he said, "if

they only knew that an American was giving orders to a member of the Italian police. I have, indeed, sold my soul to a foreign imperialist."

"Relax," I said. *"Ed elli a me, come persona accorta: 'Qui si convien lasciare ogni sospetto; ogni viltà convien che qui sia morta.' "**

"I don't want to lay down my distrust. It's insulting to have a crass American insurance detective quote Dante in the original to me." He groaned. "Oh, well ... *'E poi che la sua mano a la mia puose, con lieto volto, ond'io mi confortai, mi mise dentro a le segrete cose.' "***

I laughed. "I'll lead your way into the hidden things of a punch in the nose," I said. "Why is it any worse for me to know Dante than for a Roman detective to quote him back at me?"

"All Italians quote poetry," he said solemnly. "Besides, I was originally going to be a professor of Dante, before I discovered that under Mussolini there was more philosophy in a knife. You are disturbing, my friend. You keep bringing up the past, which is better left where it is. *'Nessum maggior dolore che ricodarsi del tempo felice nella miseria.' "****

*" 'E ció sa il tuo dottore,' "***** I said automatically. But he was right. Dante had said that the bitterest of woes is to remember old happy days. That seemed to be happening with every-

---

* A line from Dante's *Inferno,* in which the narrator is being given a tour of hell: "And he, as a person of experience, said to me: 'Here all distrust must be left aside; all cowardice must be extinguished.' "

** "And after he had laid his hand on mine, with a joyful face, which comforted me, he led my way to the hidden things."

*** "There is no greater sorrow than to remember happiness in times of misery."

**** "And this your teacher knows."

body. Wilma Pianta and Piero. But then Anna Maria probably had old happy days, too. "Besides, if you'd become a professor, you would have had a lot of students whose only interest in Dante would be as a category on that quiz show you mentioned, and you would have sat around wishing you'd become a cop."

"You're probably right, Milo."

"And you did become a cop," I said. "Or at least that's what you tell me. So go out and make like one."

"Yes, master," he said.

"Maybe we'll have the whole thing solved by the first of the week and you'll be a big hero," I said. I wasn't sure I felt that confident, but I might as well go on pretending.

"I'll depend on it, *mia papa,*" he said. The expression he was using meant father, but it was also the one Italians use in referring to the pope. The Italians have a special way of doing this sort of thing; there was no disrespect for the pope in it, but plenty for me.

*"Se non è vero, è ben trovato,"** I said.

He laughed and hung up.

The waiter had already arrived with my lunch. I ate quickly and got dressed.

Business offices would soon be closing for the afternoon, but I thought that the one I wanted to see would still be open.

I went downstairs and found a cab. I asked the driver to take me to Via Rana. He wanted to know where on the Via Rana. I said to cruise along the street until we found a wine-

* A saying usually attributed to the Renaissance philosopher Giordano Bruno: "Even if it is not true, it is well conceived."

shop. The driver was convinced that I was crazy, but he didn't argue. He was apparently accustomed to crazy Americans. We drove off.

Via Rana was quite a distance from the hotel. There was no question but that it was what might be called a slum area. The driver went slowly down the street until I finally spotted a wineshop. I told him to stop. I paid him off and got out. As I crossed the street I could feel everyone watching me out of the corner of his eye, yet nobody looked directly at me.

I found the stairway to the rooms above the wineshop, but there were no names anywhere, either downstairs or on the doors above. I went back downstairs and into the wineshop. A fat, heavily mustached man looked at me suspiciously.

"Can you tell me how to find Achille Coniglio?" I asked.

"Who wants him?" he asked me. His Italian had a heavy Sicilian accent.

"Mi chiamo Milo March." I said.

"Oh, you are the American?"

"Yes."

"Upstairs," he said, jerking his thumb toward the ceiling. "The back room on the first floor."

I thanked him and went back to climb the stairs again. I fumbled along the dark hallway until I found the last door. I knocked on it.

There was a rustling inside as though the room were infested with mice. Then it was quiet. I was about to knock again when the voice came from just the other side of the door. "Who is there?"

"Milo March," I said.

"Un minuto." I could hear a bolt being drawn. Then the voice spoke again from farther back in the room. *"Avanti."*

I opened the door and stepped inside. The room was almost as dark as the hallway, but my eyes quickly adjusted to it. It was a tiny room, crowded with two small beds, one chair, and a small table. That's all there was except for ragged clothing hanging on the walls. The remains of a loaf of bread were on the table.

Achille sat on one of the beds. A worn whetstone was in his lap, and he was carefully sharpening the blade of his knife on it. Without stopping the steady action of the blade against the stone, he stared up at me from beneath a black lock of hair.

"Che succede?" he asked.

"Nothing much," I said. "Tell me something, Achille. Last night when you were waiting in my room ... how did you know where to find me?"

"It was easy," he said. He grinned and for the first time looked boyish. "When you left the place where my brother was killed, I jumped on the back of the taxi and rode along with you. When you entered the hotel, I followed and asked one of the help for the name of the grand American. He told me. Later, after I had seen you leave, I entered the hotel and told the clerk that Signor March had asked me to call. I listened when he asked the operator for your room number. Of course you were not in and I left, but later I returned to the hotel and slipped up to your room, where I picked the lock and entered. Then I waited."

"You will probably grow up to be a very successful thief," I said dryly.

"Thank you," he said seriously. "You have found the killer of my brother?"

"Not yet, but I will, Achille."

"I have as yet no information for you," he said. "Last night it was too late to learn anything when I left you. Perhaps today ..."

"There is time," I said. "That is not why I came around."

"Then why?"

"I want to buy some other information which I'm sure that you can give me." I took out my wallet and counted out 3,000 lire. "I will pay in advance, and the other money I gave you is still an advance against other information you may get." I handed him the money.

He took the notes and handled them lovingly. "Soon I will be doing as well as my brother did," he said, "What is it that you wish to know?"

"I want to find a doctor," I said. "But not just any doctor. He should be one who doesn't have much practice, perhaps because he drinks too much. If it's not drink, it might be women or drugs. But he is one who needs money and has reached the point where he doesn't much care what he has to do to get it. There must be a few doctors like that in a city the size of Rome."

His face was old and cynical as he looked at me. "An abortion?" he asked.

"No," I said. "I haven't been in Rome that long, Achille."

"Then he would have to kill someone?"

"No. He will have to do something illegal, but it does not involve killing anyone or even helping to. If that becomes necessary, I can do my own killing."

"I believe you," he said. He was lost in thought for several minutes, his knife making a steady *thwick-thwick* on the whetstone. "There is just the man for you farther up the street," he said finally. "Cesare Teatini. I have heard people say that he was once a great doctor and surgeon. Now he is drunk all the time, except when he cannot get it, and the mothers on the street will not even let him fix a sore finger. But Stefano, who runs the wineshop downstairs, has constipation and he lets the old man give him medicine in return for wine."

"He sounds like just the man I want," I said.

"I have earned the money you gave me?"

"You have earned it, Achille." I took out cigarettes and offered him one.

When they were both lit, I said, "Tell me, Achille, you know the name Johnny Fornessi?"

"Oh, yes. Johnny Fornessi is a big man."

"In a way," I said. "Did your brother ever work for him? Or know him?"

"Many times," he said proudly. "My brother told me how many times Johnny Fornessi had to come to him and pay for information he could not get elsewhere."

"What kind of information?"

"I do not know." He hung his head. "My brother always thought I was too young."

"I understand," I said. "Brothers are like that. Was that the only kind of work your brother did for him?"

"Oh, yes. Only the information. Why?"

"I was just wondering." I stood up. "*A rivederci*, Achille."

"A rivederci," he said.

I went out and down the stairs. Before I went looking for the doctor, I searched for a place where I could buy liquor. When I found a store I bought a pint of brandy. Then I went back to find the doctor.

Dr. Cesare Teatini, according to a faded sign, was on the ground floor front of an equally faded house several doors past the wineshop. I found the door and knocked.

"Avanti," a hoarse voice called.

I opened the door and went in. I found myself in what once had obviously been a doctor's office but was no longer anything that could be so described. There was still a desk and there were marks on the floor where an examination table had once stood. There was an instrument chest with glass doors—now bare. There was a couch which was probably now a bed. The couch and the floor were well covered with newspapers.

A man was busily trying to pick up the newspapers and at the same time straighten his rumpled and greasy tie.

"Avanti, avanti," he said. "Just straightening up a bit. The last patient had a small boy—you know boys—and my nurse just happened to step out for a minute."

He looked to be in his late fifties or early sixties, and the years had not been kind to him. He had put on a lot of weight, mostly around the middle. I wasn't a doctor, but even I could guess that he probably had a liver condition. He was losing his hair, and what was left probably hadn't known a comb in days. There were deep circles under his eyes and his mouth was twitching. So were his hands, which I was sure meant he hadn't had a drink in several hours.

I went over and took a chair beside the desk and waited.

He finally got the newspapers more or less wadded into a ball, but he had no place to dispose of them. He muttered under his breath and finally shoved them into the corner at the end of the couch. He came toward me, trying not to look too eager.

"Well," he said, "what's the trouble? A little indisposition?"

"Are you Dr. Teatini?" I asked.

"Yes, yes. What seems to be wrong? By the way, my fee for office visits is ... three hundred lire. Is that too much?"

"No," I said. "If anything, it is too small. I was thinking of offering you twenty thousand lire." His mouth fell open at the amount and he seemed to be struggling for breath. I took the bottle of brandy from my pocket and set it on the edge of the desk. "With this thrown in as a gesture of good faith."

He saw the label on the bottle and one hand started forth as if by its own volition; he snatched it back and held it trembling in front of him. "Where is the young lady?" he asked.

"It's nothing like that," I said.

His tongue licked nervously at his lips, then he tore his gaze away from the bottle to look at me with eyes in which fear and desire battled. "What?" he asked.

I told him what I wanted him to do and watched while he made up his mind. It didn't take him long.

"I will do it," he said. He giggled to himself. "It is better. It will make no difference if my hands tremble. It is a bargain, Signore?"

"It is a bargain," I said.

He reached for the bottle and I pulled it away. "Where are your instruments?" I asked. "In a pawnshop?"

He nodded, then suddenly peered at me. "If you would advance me the money, I could get them before tonight."

"No," I said. "You give me the tickets and I will get the instruments. I will keep them until I come back for you tonight."

He looked disappointed, but he didn't argue. He opened a drawer in the desk. It was littered with scraps of paper, but he dug through them until he came up triumphantly with a pawn ticket. He handed it to me. His eyes were back on the bottle again.

"I'll be back for you," I said. "I want you to be able to work. That's why I brought such a small bottle. But when you're finished, you will have twenty thousand lire and you can buy a lot of bottles."

He nodded and I handed him the bottle. It was tipped to his lips as I went out the door.

I stopped at the pawnshop and picked up the instruments. On the way back to the hotel, I stopped off and bought some large test tubes and a few tools.

When I arrived at the hotel, there was a message that Signor Roccia had called twice. On the second call, he had left word that he was on his way to the hotel. I told the desk to inform him that I was in the bar when he arrived. Then I went in and ordered myself a double dry martini. I was going to need it before the night was over.

While the bartender was making the drink, I went to a phone and called the blonde. She'd been waiting to hear from me. I told her that business would keep me from seeing her that evening, but that we'd surely go to the party on the following day. She was disappointed, but she bore up under it well. I told her I was planning on renting a car to take us to the Baron's place, but she said she had a car, and it was agreed that she would pick me up the next day. I assured her that she was still the most beautiful girl in the world, and she finally let me go back to my martini. It was much more soothing.

I was working on my second double martini when Piero arrived. He slid onto the seat next to me without looking at me.

"I will have whatever the American is having," he told the bartender. "These Americans," he continued as the bartender mixed the drink. "They come over here, drink our best liquor, take our most beautiful women, and expect us to run all their errands for them."

The bartender didn't realize that we knew each other and he was embarrassed.

" 'Coverto convien che qui balli, sí che, se puoi, nascosamente accaffi,' " I said. This was also from Dante. It was the devils, pushing the barrator into the pit and telling him to cut his capers down there, to grab his secret money and pull his dirty deals in the pit.

"They even steal our best poets," Piero said dolefully.

"Put the man's drink on my bill," I told the bartender, "and we'll drink a toast to Rome—'with its sad citizens, its great company.' "*

Piero and I both laughed. The bartender, much relieved, served Piero's drink and moved down the bar to meet the demands of another thirst.

---

* Another phrase from the *Inferno*, referring to a well-populated city of hell.

"O frate mio," Piero said in delight. "One day when these matters are all finished, you and I must sit down with a large bottle between us and talk of the strange trumpeting of the demons marching along the bank of the Fifth Bolgia."*

"If we're able to sit down," I said. "In the meantime, what have you learned?"

"Americans," he said in pretended disgust. "All they think about is business. In Italy it is said that when an American dies he goes to a board of directors' meeting. Oh, well ... I spoke to the girl's parents. They swear that they have promised none of the insurance money nor has anyone asked them. I believe they are telling the truth."

"Probably," I said. "I didn't expect anything else. The Pericoloso girl was undoubtedly killed for other reasons. But I wanted to check it. What about the other thing?"

"There is something there," he said. "Giulio Ferrara lived alone at the address you gave me. He'd lived there alone since his wife died ten years ago. He was fifty-seven years old. He worked as a stonemason and worked steadily up until the day he died. He kept pretty much to himself, although he was not unfriendly with his neighbors. During the last year or so he was visited fairly regularly by a young lady. The men in the neighborhood describe her as very beautiful and roll their eyes when they say it; the women tighten their lips and say that she threw herself around too much. That will give you an idea."

"The niece?" I asked.

---

* A Bolgia is a division of Dante's Eighth Circle of Hell. This mention of the Fifth Bolgia is a reference to the corrupt politicians who dwell there.

"I don't think so. He never introduced her to anyone, and nobody in the neighborhood knew anything about his niece. I also saw the doctor who was called in when the old man died. He swears it was a heart attack that killed Ferrara."

"But there was no history, and according to the papers he had never been sick in his life."

"True," Piero said. He grinned at me. "The young lady visited Giulio the same night he died. The doctor says that there was evidence that Giulio had been engaged in man's oldest sport that night, and he thinks that's what brought on the heart attack."

"Well, he died happy," I said. "What about the niece? Did you look her up?"

"She isn't," he said.

"What?"

"There's no such person," he said. "No one named Rossana Caradonna has ever lived at the address you gave me. I did a little more checking, and there is no evidence of anyone by that name in Rome. Lots of Caradonnas, lots of Rossanas, but no Rossana Caradonna. I checked some more. Old Giulio had no brothers or sisters, therefore no direct nieces or nephews. His wife had one brother, no sisters. Her brother went to America forty years ago and has never been heard from since."

"I knew it," I said. "Where is he buried?"

He looked startled. "How the hell do I know?"

"Can you find out?"

He looked at his watch. "I guess so. You planning on joining him?"

"Any minute," I said. "Will you find out?"

"Yes, master," he said. He slid from the stool and vanished in the direction of the lobby.

I sipped my martini and waited. A bellboy came into the bar calling for Signor March. I waved him over and he handed me a cablegram. I gave him 200 lire and tore it open.

WHAT DO YOU MEAN ABOUT RING? ANSWER INSTANTER.
RAYMOND

Instanter. Now there was a Madison Avenue word for you. He probably thought he'd saved a word somewhere by using it. I folded it up and stuck it in my pocket.

Piero came back and slid onto his stool. He took a sip of his martini. "Acattolico degli Stranieri," he said.

"Isn't that the same place the Pericoloso girl is buried?" I asked.

He nodded.

"Where is it?"

"Via Caio Cestio."

I lit a cigarette and took another drink. "Let me see your hands," I said.

He held them out, palms up.

"The palms are a little soft," I remarked, "but your nerves seem steady enough. Are you officially off duty?"

"Yes." He was mystified, but he wasn't going to give me the satisfaction of asking questions.

"Then finish your drink and let's get going."

He tossed off the rest of the martini. "Where to, master?"

"Acattolico degli Stranieri," I said cheerfully. "We are about to become grave robbers."

He stared at me with his mouth open. "But—but—"

"Close your mouth, son. There are flies around this time of the year."

"Who?" he managed. "Ferrara?"

"Pericoloso," I said.

His mouth was open again. "It's—it's illegal," he said.

"Somebody told you," I said. "So is this gun I'm wearing—which you gave to me. Before this case is over we'll probably do a number of illegal things. Of course, if you're afraid ..."

He groaned. "Before this thing is over, you'll either have me made chief of the police or put in prison for life. I thought it was we Italians who were supposed to be mad."

"I believe the theory is," I said gravely, "that my mother drank Italian wine when she was carrying me." I paid the bartender. "Let's go, Piero."

"But why?" he asked as we left the bar.

"Autopsy," I said. "I've got a drunken doctor who will do it for us out of love of justice and twenty thousand lire."

"In the future," he said, "I will be careful not even to say hello to an American. It isn't safe."

We reached the lobby, where I stopped to pick up my packages. They were pretty bulky. Piero looked at them curiously but didn't ask questions until we reached the street.

"What's all that?" he asked.

"Tools of our trade," I said. "Spades, picks, flashlights, medical instruments, and test tubes."

He groaned again. "I keep hoping I'll wake up and find it's only a dream," he said.

His car was parked near the hotel. We loaded the tools into it and got started. I told him where the doctor lived.

It turned out I'd guessed about right. The doctor was a little high on the brandy I'd given him, but it was just beginning to wear off. He was just loaded enough and anxious for more to go through with the job. He bowed gravely, almost falling on his face, when I introduced him to Piero.

"You understand," he said solemnly, "I would not do this if it were not for us being old friends."

"None of us would be doing it," Piero said bitterly, "if we weren't all such old friends."

I could see the doctor studying Piero out of the corner of his eyes, probably wondering what I was paying him.

It took us a little over a half hour to reach the cemetery. It was good and dark by then. The doctor was getting a little nervy, but I was sure he still had enough liquor in him to see him through. I wasn't so sure that Piero and I did.

We parked beside the cemetery, away from the gates. We slid the tools through the fence and then we climbed over. It took a little boosting for the doctor to make it.

The grave wasn't hard to find. There was one section where they were putting all the new graves. There was already a headstone with Anna Maria's name on it. There was just enough starlight for us to see what we were doing so we wouldn't have to risk our flashlights until later.

I had brought only two shovels and two picks. I didn't want the doctor working himself into sobriety. Piero and I went to work while the doctor seated himself on the ground, humming drunkenly.

We were both out of breath when we finally reached the coffin. We carefully scraped the dirt off the top of it and raised the lid. I thrust my hand down with a flashlight in it and flicked on the light.

She had been beautiful—was even beautiful in death. She was dressed in a white satin gown, and for the first time I felt a twinge over what we were about to do. I let the beam of light glide back up to her face.

I'm not sure why I made the next move. Maybe it was only a hunch, maybe something deep in my unconscious. But I jumped down into the grave and bent over the dead girl. The smell of the grave and the undertaker's art was heavy in my nostrils and throat. I bent down, reaching into the coffin to turn the girl's head to one side. I poked the flashlight closer and stared.

"For heaven's sake, Milo," Piero said, "get out of there and let the doctor get to work and get it over with."

I let out my breath in a long sigh and straightened up. "Help me out, Piero."

He reached down his hand and I managed to leap out of the grave. Dr. Teatini was standing beside Piero, staring owlishly into the grave.

"I understand," he said, "that you want part of all the organs for examination?"

"No," I said and realized that I was breathing as hard as if I'd been running. "We don't need the autopsy after all."

"Wait a minute," the doctor said indignantly. "You promised me twenty thousand lire—"

"You'll get your money," I said. "Come on, Piero, let's get it covered up again."

We closed the lid and started shoveling dirt. It didn't take long to fill up the grave.

"Let's go," I said. "To hell with the tools. Leave them here."

"Fingerprints," Piero said quietly.

I stopped and looked at him in the starlight. "You're so right," I said. "We'll take them. I guess that's why I'd never make a good criminal. I don't have the patience." We gathered up the tools and went back the way we'd come, climbing over the fence, and got into the car. We were all silent on the drive back. The doctor because he was needing a drink badly and was probably worried about getting paid; Piero because he wouldn't ask me what I'd found as long as the doctor was with us; and I not only because of the doctor but also because seeing the girl had filled me with a nameless rage.

When we arrived in front of the doctor's place, I counted out 20,000 lire and handed them to him. I also gave him his bag of instruments.

"You are a gentleman, Signore," he said. "Are you sure there isn't some little thing I can do for you? Perhaps a prescription or—"

"No," I said curtly. "If I want anything I'll call your nurse and make an appointment."

He looked startled. "My—oh, yes. Do that by all means, Signore. *A rivederci.*" He walked off rapidly in the direction of the wineshop.

"Let's go back to the hotel," I said to Piero. "I want to get this grave smell washed off, have three or four big drinks, and maybe then I can think about such mundane things as dinner."

He sent the little Fiat shooting down the street.

"Why no autopsy?" he asked.

"There'll have to be one later," I said, "but by then maybe the police will be glad to order it. But I know how she was killed."

"How?"

"A knife. She was stabbed through the ear."

He swore.

"The family doctor can't be blamed for missing it," I said. "Any doctor would miss it unless he was doing a thorough check. All the bleeding would be internal, and there's nothing to see unless you look directly into the ear."

"What made you check it?" he asked.

"I don't really know," I said. "The informer was killed with a knife. I was wondering if it could be the same murderer. The ear is one of the few places to knife a person with some chance of its going undetected. What kind of a job was done on that informer?"

"Professional," he said. "The boys think the murderer stood behind him, cupped a hand under his chin, jerking the head up, then passed the knife across the jugular vein." We both glanced at each other.

"Yes," he said dryly. "We both saw a lot of that—once. But I don't think it means anything."

Damnit, I thought. Why were there so many things about this case reminding me of the past?

"The owner of the wineshop didn't see anything?"

"No. He was in the back, drawing wine. When he went back, Coniglio was the only person in the shop. When he came out again, that was still true, but Coniglio was dead."

"Johnny Fornessi has always been a gun artist," I said, "and so has everybody he worked with."

"That doesn't means anything," Piero said. "There are hundreds of good knife men in Rome, and most of them for hire."

"Who isn't?" I murmured. "You know that informer's kid brother, Achille?"

"A tough kid. Why?"

"I guess I thought of him now because when I met him last night he was holding a knife against my throat. And today when I went to see him—he told me about the doctor—he was whetting his knife."

"You think it means something?"

"No. He certainly didn't kill his brother—he thought at first *I* had—and when I asked him to see if he could dig up information on the Pericoloso girl, he didn't blink. He's anxious to be as successful as his brother."

"He's a tough kid," Piero said again. "I guess he's getting old enough so that we'll have to start watching him more closely."

"I like him," I said defensively. "I'd like to do something for him."

"That's only because he tried to cut your throat," Piero said with a grin. "Say, what happened about old Ferrara? I thought you wanted to dig him up, too."

"I did," I said, "but I'd had enough digging. I guess I wasn't cut out to be a grave robber. I'm a failure."

He laughed.

We were soon back at the hotel and went straight up to my room. I stripped and got into the shower, letting it run as hot as I could. When I came out I was feeling better, and for the first time the grave smell was gone from my nostrils. But I could still feel the whole experience in the pit of my stomach.

Piero stripped off and went in to use the shower. I glanced at my watch. Even though the dinner hour is late in Rome, we were well into the middle of it, but it was only late afternoon in New York. I picked up the phone and put in a person-to-person call, collect, to Martin Raymond at Intercontinental in New York.

It took three or four minutes for the call to go through, but finally he was on the phone. "Milo," he said, "what the hell's the matter with you, boy? Are you drunk?"

"Comrade Raymond," I said, "this is Comrade March, commissar of murder and other heavy industry. How go the pogroms in New York?"

"You're drunk," he said. "And crazy. How do you know who's listening in on the phone? I've been bothered by newspapermen and congressmen all day. Some senator even phoned the president of Intercontinental, and he's been on my neck all day."

"All I did was give the man an interview," I said. "Hell, you'd think I'd been playing paddleball with Bulganin all day. You ought to run down and have a Bloody Mary, or whatever they're drinking these days, and settle your dandruff. Besides, who did the planning of the Italian setup?"

"The president. It was his pet project."

"Well, he goofed."

"You were serious about that insurance ring business?" he asked. He sounded worried.

"Serious as hell," I said. "I haven't checked every one of the casualties, but I know that in one case the company paid out to a niece who never existed. I think it'll turn out that you've paid out close to one hundred and fifty grand to an insurance ring. And it's your own fault."

"The Pericoloso case one of those?"

"No," I said. "In fact, I now know that was murder—I don't know yet who the murderer is, but expect to. Anyway, it looks as if you'll have to pay the double indemnity on that one."

"All right," he said. "If we have to, we have to."

"Big of you," I said. "Which brings up a small matter. This insurance ring. That's not part of the deal and I don't feel like setting up anything on the house. What gives if I break that?"

He began to sound like a vice-president. "Look, Milo, boy, you know that we'll take care of you if you do something extra like that."

"Sure," I said. "You'll turn me over to the Activities of the Un-American Committee, or whatever it's called. Or you'll tell the visiting congressmen that maybe I am a Communist and that you'll fire me right away. I know you, buster."

"You got me all wrong, Milo. I was just kidding, just kicking the old ball around. Can't you take a joke?"

"I can take a joke when it's wrapped in dollar bills. A lot of them. How much?"

"Milo, boy, you wound me ..."

"That's no wound," I said, "that's just the place where you

spilled part of your Bloody Mary because you were loaded at lunch. I know my way around that Ulcer Gulch. How much?"

"This is all so new," he said. "I haven't touched base on it yet."

"I got news for you," I told him. "You ain't got no hits, no runs, no strikes, and no balls. Unless we agree on a price, you ain't even got a game. And don't try to correct my grammar. How much?"

"How much do you want?" he asked.

"Five thousand," I said.

"Oh, now, wait a minute. I can't—"

"If you can't," I interrupted, "you get on the other pipe and check with the president while I hold on. Get yourself wired in on this, boy, or I'll just clean up the Pericoloso case and come straight home."

"Now, wait a minute, Milo. Let's kick this around—"

"No kicking around," I said firmly. "Look, buster, you've paid off one hundred and fifty grand on one hundred and ninety-three stiffs. You have to stop it now or you're out of business. If you have to ask upstairs, go ahead. I'll hold on."

"At transatlantic rates?"

"At transatlantic rates."

"That's a pretty stiff price, Milo."

"I'm trying to prove I'm not a Communist," I said. "It's your nickel, buster. Make up your mind."

"All right," he said with a sigh. "We'll pay you five thousand if you crack it. You drive a hard bargain, Milo."

"I drive anything that has wheels," I said. "And you've got wheels, Comrade Raymond. In your head. Give my love to the congressmen." I hung up.

I turned around to find Piero standing behind me. He was rubbing himself with a towel and grinning at me. "That was the man you work for?" he asked.

I nodded.

"You make me feel better," he said. "I thought it was only cops you jumped on. Now that I know it's everyone, I'm happier."

"I didn't know you understood English," I said.

"A little," he said. "Last year one of your Hollywood actresses was over here and had her jewelry stolen. I was assigned to the case."

"Did you find the jewels?"

"Not exactly. But I found a lot of other things—including an understanding of some English."

"That doesn't explain how you understood me," I said. "I wasn't using any of those words. Let's get moving, Piero."

We were soon both dressed and went downstairs again. At Piero's suggestion, we had a fast drink in the bar and then we went to the oldest quarter of the city, Trastevere. The restaurant we ate at was rich with the smells of red wine, spicy cooking, and strong tobacco. It was a low-ceilinged room with bare wooden tables. The waiters were all in their shirtsleeves. A woman was wandering around among the tables playing a guitar while her little daughter tagged along behind, singing. It was a lot better than the places Gianna had taken me the night before. I began to get hungry.

We ordered Spaghetti alla Carbonara, which is made with a hot sauce of bacon, egg, and pepper, and a large bottle of Valpolicella. It was a hell of a good meal.

"Tomorrow you move into high society," Piero said while we were eating. "You got a plan?"

I shook my head. "I don't like to clutter things up," I said. "Truthfully, I don't have a plan. I'll have to play it by ear. But something about this whole mess has been playing around in my head. You say you think that Baron Gambero and Johnny Fornessi have been doing business in drugs?"

"We're positive of it, but we can't prove it."

I nodded. "I don't know how we're going to pin the murder on them, but maybe we can do something. What's your general idea on the drug traffic?"

"We think they're getting it from the East by boat—most of it probably raw opium from Red China. We think they store it on Gambero's estate and maybe work the raw opium into heroin and then ship it on to America and to other parts of Europe. We've watched the place a lot without getting anywhere."

"You think young Balena is part of it?"

"I doubt it. Gambero and young Balena have a real estate business together. I think I told you he makes a practice of going into legitimate businesses with the sons of important men. I don't think Riccardo Balena is in the drug business. At the same time, by being around, the Pericoloso girl may have learned something and that might be the reason they killed her. I doubt if they'd kill her just because the boy was tired of her."

"I think you're right," I said. I thought about it for a minute. "Gambero gives a lot of parties?"

"Yes. Big ones. I'm told there are never less than fifty people at them, often more."

"Did it ever occur to you that those parties would be the perfect time for them to bring in the drugs? A boat could come in and it would look like guests arriving for the party."

He stopped eating to stare at me. "We never did think of that," he said slowly. "We've had men out there when parties are going on, but we never took the risk of searching arriving guests. Maybe you have something, Milo."

"You have authority out there?" I asked.

He nodded. "You forget that I am a part of the national police, not just the city of Rome. We are more like your FBI."

"Good," I said. "Another thing: if I'm right, it's only half of it. I assume that you've tried searching his estate?"

"Dozens of times."

"So the other half of it is where he keeps the stuff. Is there a landing for his estate?"

"Yes. At the foot of a steep hill. There is a stairway for guests."

"My idea," I said, "is for you to be out there. We can arrange to meet at the foot of the hill by the landing. You stay out of sight until I get a lead. Then you can come in. We're due out there tomorrow afternoon. I'll contact you tomorrow night. If I haven't uncovered anything by then, I'll meet you again on Sunday. Between the two of us, we ought to be able to stir up something."

"Good," he said.

"I've got a hunch we'll break it open this weekend," I said. "If nothing else, that interview I gave the Communist paper will make them nervous. Well, we'll see."

He nodded and we finished eating. After the spaghetti, we

had creamy Gorgonzola cheese with pear. It was the perfect ending to the meal. On the way back to the hotel, we stopped off at the Ristorante Passetto and had a couple of brandies. Then we drove on and Piero dropped me at the hotel. It was agreed we would meet at the landing the following night.

I went straight upstairs to my room. I unlocked the door and stepped inside. I had closed the door and was feeling for the light switch.

"Why bother with the light?" a voice said. The voice was soft and throaty.

It took me a minute to place it. What helped was the scent in the room. It was the same scent that had been on my pillow that afternoon.

I turned and walked across the dark room.

FIVE

It was late when I awakened the following morning. There was nothing to remind me of the night before except a faint lingering scent on the pillow next to mine. Except for that I was alone and it might as well have been a dream. I lit a cigarette and lay there thinking of various kinds of madness. In its own way, this was the most peculiar case I'd ever been on. Nothing had really happened on it, but every time I looked at it there was something, and there was the feeling that at any minute it was going to explode. And there were so many things about it that brought up the past. Wilma Pianta, Piero, even Achille Coniglio. The result was that I felt I was living half in the past and half in the present. Even Baron Gambero was part of this; he represented the enemy of the past, and I found myself convicting him in my mind without any evidence against him.

There was more. I was well aware of the tightrope that I was walking. The murder of a girl, the deaths (murder, I was sure) of 193 policyholders—all of these things could overthrow an entire government because of one boy who was lost in a world of changing values and was consequently wild. Despite my scorn for their methods, I shared the concern of the man from the American Embassy, Piero, and all the others who were afraid that the Christian-Democrat government would topple and give the Communists the break they were looking for. There was only one difference. I felt that nothing was ever accomplished by hiding things; if you look hard enough for justice in one direction, you may find it everywhere. I felt that even if Riccardo Balena was guilty, his father and the government could ride that out better than they could the whispers that never stopped.

I was well aware that upon that belief hung the fate of the Italian government—as well as my own.

Even with his fate in the balance, a man needs food. I picked up the phone and ordered some breakfast. Then I had a quick shower and shaved before they brought it.

After breakfast I had a good shot of brandy. That would have horrified Martin Raymond, but I'm not one of those fussy people. If brandy is good after dinner, it's just as good after breakfast. Maybe a little better.

Having some time to kill, I took the gun from the holster and checked it over to make sure it was working. It was.

The phone rang. I picked it up and said hello.

"This is Achille," the voice on the other end said. "I just phoned to tell you that today I really go to work getting information for you. I will call you the minute I have something."

"Fine, Achille," I said. "But I won't be here until late on Sunday. I'm leaving very shortly."

"You are leaving Rome?"

"Only for the weekend. I'm going down to the estate of Baron Gambero. I'll be back Sunday night."

"You are taking a short rest?" he asked politely.

"No rest," I told him. "There is a big party there, but I am going to look for the killer of the girl and your brother."

"Oh."

"I'll see you when I get back," I said. *"A rivederci."*

"A rivederci," he said. I had the feeling that he wanted to say more, but he left it at that. The phone clicked and I put the receiver down.

A few minutes later the desk called up to say that Signorina Bionda was downstairs for me. I said I'd be right down. I was already dressed and had packed the things I'd need. All I had to do was close the lid of the suitcase and go.

Gianna was waiting in the lobby. She was wearing a light blue dress that set off her blond good looks. I noticed the usual cleavage was there. I wasn't sure I would have recognized her if it hadn't been.

"All ready?" she asked gaily.

It was a silly question. "No," I said. "I just came down to see if you were dressed yet."

She gave me that laugh again and everybody in the lobby started looking to see if Bob Hope had come in. I took her by the arm and steered her out of the hotel before they could discover he hadn't.

She was driving a little Porsche. It was a beautiful car and would have thrilled the heart of many an American, but cars like that always leave me feeling that I'm about to start walking any minute. We stored my suitcase in the back with hers and got in.

I was surprised. She turned out to be a good driver and after a few blocks I was able to relax—except for that feeling about walking.

Not only did she drive well, but she managed to do it while

chattering just as much as she did when she wasn't driving. Before we were out of the city I had her life story and she was beginning a rundown on all the plays and movies in which she had appeared. Italian movies are fine to see once in a while, but when you start hearing the plots one after another, you get the feeling that Italy is made up of nothing but shoeshine boys and prostitutes. It's a wonder that they ever get any faces in the pictures.

Out of the city, we were soon following a road near the sea, bordered with scraggly pine trees that looked as if they were stage props from those same Italian movies.

Within a half hour we were going through Ostia. It looked like Coney Island with Italian signs. As we left it, I watched the beach, wondering which spot of sand had held Anna Maria's body.

Gianni was telling me about her fifth—or maybe it was the sixth—role as the prostitute with the heart of gold. I guess I'd always known the wrong kind of streetwalkers. The ones I'd known had a more practical idea about the source of gold.

Another half hour—and three more prostitute roles—and we hit Torvaianica. It was a sleepy little village right on the sea—the kind of place you'd like to retire to, if you were eighty.

"Isn't the Baron's place near here?" I asked, interrupting her story about the director who thought she had a more perfect body than any actress in Italy.

"It's a little more than a mile from here," she said. "I hope I haven't been boring you with the story of my career."

If that one part was all she was ever going to play, it wasn't a career, it was a profession.

"Not at all," I said gallantly. "I found it very interesting."

"After all," she said, "if you're going to be interested in my career, you should know everything about me."

"Everything," I agreed gravely. "In fact, I've been waiting for you to tell me about the one dimple—I've forgotten now, is it on the left or the right hip?"

She looked at me, her brow furrowed with thought. "You are joking, aren't you?"

"Rather lamely," I admitted.

"Because," she went on, "I have dimples on both hips. You don't think that will spoil my career in Hollywood, do you?"

"If anything, it will enhance it," I said seriously. "In fact, I'm told there is one producer in Hollywood who won't hire an actress until he's affirmed the presence of at least one dimple. He even has a letter from his doctor saying that the sight of such dimples is vital to his health. I heard that his test shots are the most interesting in Hollywood."

She looked at me again, then gave up trying to decide whether I was joking or not. She picked up the thread of her story where I had caused her to drop a stitch.

A mile or so below Torvaianica, she turned off on a narrow road to the right and sent the Porsche hurtling up the hill.

I'll have to say this for Gianna: she had a wonderful sense of timing. She managed to bring the story of her life right up to the point where she'd met me just as we pulled in to what was obviously the Baron's estate.

It was quite a joint even from the distance of the parking lot. Any American suburban dweller would have had trouble recognizing the house as such. It was more of a castle. As an offhand guess, I would say it had at least eighty rooms. There were a number of lesser dwellings scattered around, any one of which would have served as a mansion for a plain millionaire. At a farther distance there were what seemed to be stables and garages. The main house was surrounded by landscaped grass and flower beds with a few modest statues and fountains. Around at the back of the house there was a swimming pool.

A number of guests were apparently already there. There were quite a few cars in the large parking area, most of them sports cars.

"Are you sure he has room for us?" I asked, looking at the house. "If he's crowded, I could always sleep in the car."

She giggled.

We'd barely parked when a servant showed up. He went around to the back and took out the luggage. He looked at Gianna.

"Signorina Bionda and Signor March," he said. He marched off with the luggage, having proved that he was well trained.

Gianna giggled again. "Baron Gambero is very intelligent about these parties," she said. "He will have given us adjoining rooms."

"With our names on them, I hope," I said brightly. "I'd hate to make a mistake. I don't think I'd look my best showing up for breakfast in one of your dresses."

"Silly," she said. She took my arm and we started for the house—quite a hike. I thought it was unsporting of the Baron not to provide some sort of transportation from car to house. Something like giant turtles with jewel-encrusted backs.

"What's the routine here?" I asked her as we walked to the house. "Do we all play charades or just stand around pulling at our forelocks whenever the Baron approaches?"

"The guests will be coming all afternoon and during the evening," she said, "so this afternoon everything will be very informal. There will be drinks and food, and everybody just mixes around and becomes acquainted. During dinner tonight there will be music and afterwards a show. Sometimes he brings singers and dancers from as far as Paris. Tomorrow there will be a late, informal breakfast. If it's a nice day, there will be swimming and tennis afterwards. Then in the afternoon all the men go boar hunting and there's a prize for the man who kills the largest boar. After that the party begins breaking up slowly."

"All the men go in for boar hunting?" I asked.

She nodded. "It's a regular feature of the parties."

"Why should I shoot a boar?" I demanded. Personally, my own feeling about anyone who went big-game hunting was that the man was merely trying to use a gun to prove what he felt he hadn't been able to prove in a bedroom.

She laughed. "You're funny," she said. "The Baron always has the boar hunts. He says that it's an old tradition in his family. He says they've been doing it for centuries."

"Boar hunting, like charity," I muttered, "begins at home. Maybe he should just look in a mirror."

She stared at me. She didn't get it. "Don't you want to go boar hunting?" she asked.

"I'm panting to," I said. That was, I must confess, a small exaggeration. I don't like vice-presidents, but I'm strictly a Madison Avenue boy myself. My idea of roughing it is when you have to drink gin straight instead of in a martini. "Where's he get all the boars?"

"They just grow here. He's got more than a thousand acres, and there are hundreds and hundreds of wild boars in the forest. He says that the hunts are necessary to keep them from taking over the place."

"I'll bet," I said, "that nobody looked at it from the pigs' viewpoint. Think how the poor sow feels when her husband doesn't come home from a hard day among the acorns. What do we do with them after we kill them—rip at the flesh with bared fangs?"

"Oh, you," she said. "I think he gives most of them to the servants. But he always sends two or three of them to some convent—it's his favorite charity."

"How sisterly of him," I said. "What's the prize for the biggest boar?"

"A case of champagne and a champagne cup engraved like a loving cup. I think it's cute."

"That's the only word for it," I agreed solemnly. "What about young Balena? He looked as if he wasn't too pleased about your being with me."

"I've been out with him a few times," she said as we reached the house, "and I guess he's the kind who thinks he owns a girl. He's just a silly boy."

"Aren't we all?" I said. "Did you know his previous girlfriend, Anna Maria Pericoloso?"

"No," she said. "I heard about her drowning on the beach. I thought it was simply terrible. I think it must be a terrible way to die."

"Damp," I agreed as we arrived at the door.

The butler must have been watching through the keyhole, for he opened the door at the precise moment we arrived. He looked like an ambassador from a minor European country.

We walked into the house. It wasn't too much different from the Metropolitan Museum. It was filled with antiques—furniture, tapestries, paintings, even some of the guests. We walked through a couple of rooms to reach the one that seemed to be the place for the gathering of the clan. It was a huge room, large enough to house several families—also large. A huge table was set up with various kinds of foods both hot and cold. At one end there was a bar, only slightly larger than the one at the Waldorf, with three bartenders at the alert. There were probably about twenty people there, milling around and trying to look as if they were having the time of their lives.

Baron Gambero showed up just as we entered the room. He looked even more like an undertaker than when I'd first met him.

"So glad you could come," he murmured. He took Gianna's hand and kissed it. I was getting ready to slug him if he tried the same thing with me, but he didn't even offer to shake my hand.

"So happy to have our distinguished American visitor," he said to me. He was examining me with about as much expression as a pair of eyes in the Fulton Fish Market. "I understand you've been having a little publicity since arriving in Rome."

I noticed that young Balena had come up behind him and was watching me with what in my circle would have been known as the evil eye. "You know how it is," I said. "I'm a stranger in town and so I try to be nice when a reporter starts talking to me. I didn't know he was a Communist. I don't know much about politics. I wouldn't know a Christian-Democrat from a Fascist even if I saw them standing together." I stared at the two of them as innocently as I could.

"It is difficult to be in a strange country," the Baron said smoothly. It was impossible to tell if he meant any threat in it. "It is true that you are interested in the fate of that poor girl?"

"Very true," I said.

"We knew her, you know," he said. He looked at young Balena, and it seemed to me that there was a hint of cruelty in his face. "Riccardo was once very fond of her."

"I just knew her, that was all," Riccardo said sullenly.

"In the Biblical meaning?" I asked.

Young Balena's face grew an angry red, and the Baron looked amused.

"I think it is terrible, the way she drowned and everything," Gianna said.

The Baron looked at her briefly. "It is always terrible when a beautiful woman dies," he said. His gaze came back to me. "You really think she was murdered, Signore?"

"Definitely," I said.

For a minute I had the impression he was staring at me through a lorgnette.

"What do you intend to do about it?" he asked.

"The usual thing," I said. "Get the one who did it."

"Really? How quaint. I think this is the first time I've ever had a man hunter here as my guest. You should enjoy the boar hunt tomorrow."

"I suppose there is a certain similarity," I said.

"He may not enjoy it so much," Riccardo Balena said. "The boars can fight back."

"So can the others," I said.

"Signor March is right," Baron Gambero said, "as I'm sure he always is. Tell me, Signore, I know about the boar hunting, but what weapon do you use in your sport?"

"I prefer to use my brains," I said.

"A small arms man," Riccardo said with a sneer.

"Quiet, boy," the Baron said without looking around. "I am sorry that I must be the host now, Signore, but we must talk about this another time."

"Any time," I said. "Only the subject is apt to get a little rough. I suggest that we hold the conversation anywhere except the nursery. ... Let's go get one of those drinks, Gianna."

I took her by the arm and we walked past them. The Baron was still looking amused, while young Balena looked as if he might have a stroke any minute.

"What was that all about?" Gianna asked.

"Jokes."

"It didn't sound like jokes."

"A new kind of joke," I explained. "The Baron and I are forerunners in it."

"But I thought you didn't know each other until I introduced you night before last."

"We didn't, but we recognized our kinship immediately. What will you have to drink, dear?"

"Whatever you suggest."

We reached the bar and I gave the matter some thought. I finally decided on Bloody Marys. But that brought up another problem; how to ask for them in Italian. The nearest I could come to it was something like *Sangue Maria,* but I knew that wasn't right. Finally, I settled for telling the bartender how to make them. He had a little trouble finding tomato juice, but he finally managed and under my guidance he made a fairly good Bloody Mary.

"I like it," Gianna said when she tasted the drink. "You are so clever, Milo."

"I have my traditions and the Baron has his," I said modestly.

We had a couple more drinks at the bar. Gianna turned to wave at several people. Finally she tugged at my sleeve and said she wanted me to come meet some people. I wasn't quite up to meeting the Baron's guests, so I told her to go ahead and I'd join her in a few minutes. I had another Bloody Mary and then with a fresh one in my hand I turned around to consider the other guests.

More people must have arrived while I was contemplating the advantages of a well-stocked bar. There were now close to forty people in the room, roaming around with drinks in their hands or nibbling at bits of food. For the most part, they tended to cluster in small groups of four or five. I recognized a couple of Italian movie stars, and over in one corner of the room there was a well-known Hollywood starlet. I didn't recognize any of the other girls, but they were cast in pretty much the same mold. The men, on the other hand, averaged about twenty years older than the girls, and most of them looked like prosperous businessmen or aging playboys. The only older women present were ones who were obviously loaded with money, and around them the few young men present danced attendance.

Large double doors on the far side of the room had been thrown open on a terrace and the pool beyond. A few people were on the terrace.

Gianna stood with a small group of people, but at the moment was engaged in what seemed to be a heated conversation with Riccardo Balena. Then I spotted someone else I knew. Mr. Albert Blaine, the man from the American Embassy, stood at one end of the table by himself. He was gnawing delicately on a piece of fish. He had a drink in his hand, but he was holding it as if it might explode. I grinned and made my way over to him.

"Haven't we met before?" I asked gravely. "Your face looks familiar."

He wasn't amused. "Hello, March," he said. "By the way, I meant to ask you yesterday, how did you get invited here?"

"A very good question," I said. "I was wondering myself. To be perfectly truthful, I owe it all to the little woman." I indicated Gianna, who was standing not far away. "For some reason she thinks insurance companies have influence with the Hollywood movie companies, and she is hoping that I will get her into movies. So she persuaded the Baron to invite us together."

"You do get around, don't you?" he said, after a brief glance at the blonde. "She is usually the constant companion of the young man to whom she is talking."

"The son of the Minister of the Interior," I murmured. "It seems that politics gets into everything, doesn't it?"

"Yes," he said. He looked at me, and for the first time I saw something like a human expression in his eyes. "You might be interested in knowing that I had two phone calls about you just before I left Rome today."

"I'm just naturally popular," I said. "It comes from leading a clean life. I hope you didn't give out my phone number. I do have to limit my social activities."

"The first call," he said, "was made by an undersecretary of the Department. While he said that I should continue to keep a sharp eye on you, he also indicated that I was to do it gently and that there was probably a mistake in your being quoted by the Communist press."

"Sweet of him," I murmured.

"The first call was made at six in the morning, New York time," he said. "The second call came a half hour later. It was from J. P. Walker in New York. We're old friends. I don't think he's been up at six-thirty in the morning in twenty years, so he must have been up all night thinking about the call. He wanted to tell me that you are a very valuable man and that you are the victim of a grave political misunderstanding. He wanted me to give you every assistance I could."

I grinned. J. P. Walker is the president of Intercontinental. I'd never met him but I knew who he was. He was also a very rich man, and a man who was active in American politics. So active that it was well known that he could have had a cabinet post if he'd wanted it. I guessed that Martin Raymond must have had a talk with him after my phone call the day before.

"Who the hell are you, March?" Blaine asked irritably. "I've never known anyone to get away with the kind of stuff you pull and have pulled."

"My father was actually the Lost Dauphin of France," I said earnestly. "By the way, aren't you supposed to be interested in what happens to American businessmen in Italy?"

"I'm interested in all our nationals," he said. "What are you driving at?"

"J. P. Walker. The Intercontinental Italian company is his baby. He has dreams of becoming an international insurance cartel. And he's started out by taking a royal rooking."

"What do you mean?"

"He's been taken by an insurance ring in Rome."

"How do you know this?"

"I know," I said. "At this minute, I don't know about every single one of them, but I'll bet that one hundred and ninety-three citizens of Rome have been persuaded to take out insurance and then have been murdered so that the ring could collect the dough."

"My God," he said. "Is the Pericoloso case part of this?"

"No," I said. "That's a different dish of tea. But she was murdered, too. And I wouldn't say that the murders aren't related."

"Look, March," he said, lowering his voice, "I don't give a damn who you are or who says to handle you gently. If these things are true, don't jump in like a romantic fool and try to show off by clearing everything up. You'll be stirring up things nobody can fix."

"Watch that blood pressure, Dad," I told him, "or you'll

never live to collect your pension. Don't worry about it. The national police are already in on it, even if they don't know it."

He looked at me intently. "Roccia?" he asked.

"What makes you ask that?" I countered.

"I know you were with him last night and the night before. I told you that we were keeping an eye on you."

"Were you watching all the time last night?" I asked.

"No. Why? What were you up to?"

"Just digging up some dirt," I said truthfully. "Just relax. Your fate is in good hands."

His face got darker with congested blood, but he remembered to keep his temper.

"By the way," I said, "what are you doing at this clambake?"

"I told you that I would be watching you," he said. "I usually attend these parties anyway. As you will see, there will be at least two Ministers here and representatives from most of the big embassies. Baron Gambero is an important man. Not many people refuse invitations to his parties."

"Important in the neo-Fascist party?" I asked.

"He is important in many ways," he said evasively. "You'll find all sorts of people here. I expect even your Communist friend will show up this afternoon."

I happened to look up just then and saw who was arriving. It was Johnny Fornessi. The beautiful brunette was with him.

"You mean people like him?" I asked.

Blaine looked and nodded. "Even him," he said. "He's nearly always here. You seem to know quite an assortment of people, March."

"So do you," I said cheerfully. "Tell me, Blaine, how do you stand on the question of this wild boar hunting jazz?"

"It's a pleasant sport," he said.

"Who isn't?" I retorted. I moved off toward the bar, I needed another Bloody Mary. When I had it, I turned away, only to find myself face to face with Johnny Fornessi.

"Well," I said, "they must have scraped the bottom of the barrel for the guests at this party."

"Hello, Milo," he said. He gave me a malicious grin. "Been doing any sightseeing lately?"

"No. I've been afraid that somebody might get his throat cut if I did."

His grin grew broader. "You're not going to try to pin that on me, are you? You're the one guy who knows that I didn't have anything to do with that."

"Sure," I said. "I guess you're not working with Lucky Topo these days, are you?"

"I see Lucky once in a while, but that's all. I'm not even working myself. Why?"

"Well, I remember," I said, "when you used to work with Lucky and people were always getting mysteriously shot. Now when you're around, people seem to get knifed. So I figured you'd changed boys."

"You cops are all alike," he said. "You figure I'm to blame for everything."

"Not a clean-living boy like you, Johnny," I said. "Go get yourself drunk. I'll be seeing you around."

I wandered across the room. The girl who had come with Johnny was standing alone and on an impulse I started toward her. This was the first time I'd taken a good look at her. There was something familiar about her. Then I drew nearer and the scent she was wearing tugged at my senses.

It was almost like a physical blow. I stopped and stared, and I could see it. I had never seen her with makeup on, or dressed like this, but I had seen her with her hair down and with the glasses off. I had seen that she was beautiful, but I hadn't thought of her as the girl with Johnny Fornessi—or even a girl that I would meet in any nightclub.

"Hello," she said. Her voice again had that soft quality that I'd heard in it only the night before in my room.

I stood and looked at her. Even though I'd had plenty of evidence that she was beautiful, it was still hard to realize that this was the mousy-looking woman who worked in the Intercontinental office.

"I don't get it," I said shaking my head.

"You mean my being with Johnny Fornessi?" she asked. She shrugged her shoulders. "It's really very simple. He spends a lot of money, and I like to go places."

"I didn't mean that," I said. "I long ago gave up trying to figure out why girls go with some of the men they do. I was talking about this double personality. The Wilma Pianta in the office and this Wilma Pianta. Or do you have another name to go with this personality?"

She laughed. "I'm still Wilma Pianta," she said. She reached out and touched my hand with her fingers and that strange current of feeling was between us again. She laughed again, with pleasure. "It's just that when I'm in an office, I feel like that Wilma Pianta. It also makes life much simpler. If I looked like this all the time, I would have more trouble in any office where I happened to work."

"I suppose so," I admitted.

One thing was certain, I was having to revise my ideas about her. I'd have to give up the picture of her standing in front of her mirror and remembering the glamour she'd once had. But it seemed to me that she was still living in the past. In a way, that would explain the two quite different personalities. Then she must have lived her days lost in the shuffle of Roman crowds, just another pretty girl; but at night she became La Ragazza and someone pretty special. In a way, that must be what she was still doing.

"Leave my girl alone," Johnny Fornessi said, coming back with two drinks, "or I'll get my new boy after you." He laughed.

"I am not your girl," Wilma said levelly. I had the feeling that she was saying it mostly for my benefit. "I like going out with you, Johnny, but that does not make me your girl."

"Broads," Johnny said to me in English. "They always have to yak about something."

"Well," I said, "be happy kids." I waved and walked off to find Gianna. Still more people had arrived and the room was filling up. I soon found her, and young Balena was no longer with her. She pouted when she saw me.

"I thought you had deserted me," she said.

"Not a chance, honey," I said. "I was just waiting for you to get through with Riccardo."

"He annoys me," she said.

"Come on," I said. "I want to look this joint over. Give me a guided tour."

We left our glasses on the table and went out on the terrace. It was quite a backyard. The swimming pool looked as if somebody had put three Hollywood pools together. There were three tennis courts and a badminton court—all of them deserted. The Baron's guests didn't seem to go in for any athletics except elbow bending.

We walked around the back of the house and past a number of pleasant little houses, which Gianna said were the servants' quarters. Then we came to another building that looked large enough to be someone's house, but Gianna said it was the freezer. My idea of a freezer had always been something like a refrigerator. I went over and opened the door. It was a freezer, all right. There was enough food in it to feed a small army.

Another building almost as large turned out to be a wine cellar and liquor storage house. The Baron was all set for a long, hard winter. Then there was a gun building, filled with all kinds of fancy guns. For the boar hunting, I guessed. Next we saw the stables where the Baron had twenty blooded horses. And the garages. His six cars were just as blooded as the horses; the smallest thing in it was a Jaguar.

On the other side of the stables and garages there was a fence, and beyond it the beginning of woods.

"I've never been in there," Gianna said, "but I hear that it's like a real jungle with all kinds of animals in it."

"Including wild boars," I said. I was beginning to feel persecuted by those boars without having seen them.

She laughed. "This is about all of it, except inside the house," she said. "There are hundreds and hundreds of acres in the woods. You want to see the house?"

"What, no yacht basin?" I asked.

"Oh, yes. You want to see it?"

"I'm dying to," I said. It was the one thing I did want to see, since that was where I would be meeting Piero later.

We walked around the side of the house to the front. There was a wide, flower-bordered walk leading down to the cliff overlooking the sea. We followed it to the cliff edge. A flight of stairs led down the hundred or so feet to the beach. Three boats were docked below, and a fourth one, only a little smaller than a liner, was docking. To the left of the dock there was a huge private beach, the sand gleaming whitely in the sunlight. A fence separated it from the dirtier-looking beach beyond.

There wasn't much room for concealment down there, but at night it would probably be safe to meet on the beach.

The yacht had docked, and three men and a woman had gotten off and were starting up the stairs.

"You want to go down?" Gianna asked.

"I guess not," I said. "I'm not as young as I used to be."

"Silly," she said.

I was watching the four new guests. In most ways they certainly looked like the rest of Baron Gambero's guests, yet it seemed to me that in some way they were different. I finally decided it was only their manner; they didn't look quite so indolent as most of the people back in the house.

They reached the top of the stairs and looked curiously at us. "Hello," the woman said. Her Italian was accented, but I couldn't tell what sort of accent it was. The men with her nodded.

Gianna and I said hello and they went on past us. Looking after them, I saw that Baron Gambero was coming out to meet them.

I looked back down at the yacht. Three crewmen were coming off the boat, each of them carrying a large box on his shoulder. They started up the stairs.

Gianna and I walked slowly back toward the house. When we were almost up to where the Baron stood with his latest guests, I stopped her. We were beside one of the fountains. It was ringed with flowers. I stepped over and plucked one of the flowers. I came back and handed it to Gianna.

"That was sweet of you," she said.

"I'm the sweet type," I muttered. I was watching the three crewmen. They'd reached the top of the cliff and were walking toward the back of the house. I watched them, wondering what was in the boxes. I would have given anything to have taken a look inside one of them. I had a hunch that I might have found raw opium.

From the way they were heading, it looked as if they were going to the building that Gianna had said was the wine cellar.

"You like my little place?" a voice said behind me.

I turned around. Baron Gambero had come up behind us while I was watching the three men. I knew that he must have seen me watching the men, and I found it interesting that he'd picked this time to come over and be friendly.

"Not bad," I said. "You must have at least three or four lots here."

He gave a bleak smile. "One thousand, two hundred and

fifty acres," he said. "It has been in my family for one thousand years."

"It's a good thing you kept up with the taxes," I told him. "It would be tough to have to pay them all at once."

Gianna was trying unobtrusively to catch my eye so she could signal me to go easy. I knew what she wanted, but I ignored her. I didn't particularly care whether the Baron liked me or not.

"You are a very refreshing personality, Signor March," he said. He saw me looking to where the three men were entering the wine cellar. "You are interested in what my guests have brought me?"

"Not especially," I said. "It's probably not in my line."

"I don't imagine it is," he said. His tone might have been a threat and it might not. "These last arrivals are very dear friends of mine. They have recently returned from Japan and they brought me some sake."

"Sake?" Gianna said.

"Japanese whiskey," I told her. "Three drinks of it and you get slant-eyed."

"A rough but accurate description," the Baron said. "I am planning a Japanese party next month. If you are still in Rome, Signor March, you must come."

"I'd love to," I said. I looked at him. "I've even got a suggestion for you. Why not hold the party at the Queen of Heaven?" I knew—and I was sure he did—it was the name for Rome's oldest prison.

He knew, but he didn't blink an eye. "A very amusing suggestion," he said. "I must speak to one of my friends in the government about it."

"I'm sure it could be arranged," I told him.

"I will consider it," he said thoughtfully. "Well, I am most happy that you are enjoying yourself, Signor March." He turned and marched back to the house.

"I don't get it," Gianna said. "It sounded to me like you were needling him."

"It's an old March tradition," I said. "We don't like barons. And that's been in my family for one thousand years. Come on and show me the house. I'm beginning to need a drink."

We went into the house and she showed me the downstairs rooms. There was a game room, a billiard room, a library, an art gallery, and a meditation room. The last, so help me, had stained-glass windows. There was also a small theater and, of course, the dining room where several huge tables were already set.

When we'd seen them, we went back to the drinking room, with me urging her on to a faster gait. The bartender remembered me when he saw me coming through the crowd and he had a Bloody Mary all ready by the time I got there. He won my undying gratitude by that simple gesture.

The place had really filled up. There must have been close to a hundred people there. Among them I saw at least one more face I recognized. Ugo Marrone, the Communist.

As soon as Gianna had her drink, we started circulating. Every so often, she'd pull at my arm and introduce me to someone. During the next few minutes I met politicians, minor royalty, a movie producer, a jockey, an opera singer, and a number of people who didn't seem to do anything but spend money. I noticed that Gianna was careful not to introduce me to any of the other actresses in the room.

The next couple of hours went by in that fashion. I got a little bit loaded, but so did everybody else. In fact, some of them got quite a bit loaded. The conversations I managed to listen in on sounded pretty dull. A few times while we were circulating, I ran into Albert Blaine as well as Johnny Fornessi and Wilma Pianta. Once I encountered Ugo Marrone. Before I could duck, he'd grabbed my hand and thanked me for my great help.

"We'll soon have the lid off the whole mess," he said to me in a tone that implied we were fellow conspirators.

"We?" I asked. "You couldn't find a crook even if you were turned loose in the Kremlin."

I think he was going to say something nasty in return, but I was gone before he could get the dialectics worked out.

Finally it was announced that dinner was ready and we all went into the dining room. Off in another room a small orchestra was playing soft music. The dining room was lit by candles only, which made all the women look better and the men worse. I've never understood why candlelight should do this, but it does.

I was sitting between Gianna and some horse-faced woman who was loaded with diamonds. They were so big and bright they almost put the candles out. She was wearing a gown that was meant to show cleavage, but despite her best efforts it was more like droopage. It also turned out that all she wanted to talk about was Monte Carlo and had I been to the wedding.* After that I gave all my attention to Gianna. She wasn't much to talk to, but at least the view was good.

* The wedding of Grace Kelly to Prince Rainier III of Monaco in April of 1956.

The Baron set quite a table. There was enough food on it to feed five hundred, and you would have had to stop and think in order to ask for something that wasn't there. There were four or five kinds of wine, all of them perfection. Afterwards, with the coffee, there was brandy that must have been almost as old as the Baron's estate.

Everybody ate and drank and talked at once, and the place was bedlam.

When dinner was finally over, we all straggled into the theater. Now we were going to get the singing and dancing. I managed to make sure that Gianna and I sat well toward the back.

As soon as we were all seated, the show started. The first act opened my eyes. The Baron's show was going to be nothing but a high-class burlesque show. Maybe not so high-class at that.

A well-stacked redhead was busily proving the obvious and I hated to miss it, but this was my chance. I slipped out of my seat without even Gianna's knowing I was leaving.

I went out the front way and lingered for a couple of minutes by the fountain to be sure that no one was following me. When I was certain, I walked out to the cliff and went down the stairs. It was a dark night. The only light came from the riding lights on the boats and the stars. The starlight made the waves sparkle like a million small diamonds.

I wasn't sure exactly where to meet Piero, but I thought it wouldn't be too close to the dock. I walked down along the beach. When I got near enough to the fence to see it, I stopped and lit a cigarette. Then I walked on slowly.

As I reached the fence, I became aware of a shadowy figure leaning against it.

"Piero?" I said softly.

"Yes," he said. "I was wondering how long it would take you to get here. How are things up there?"

"They're all watching a bunch of strippers. I hope you realize how loyal I am to come out at a time like that."

"I shall recommend the medal of valor," he said. "Have you learned anything yet?"

"Not a thing except that the Baron's parties make stranger bedfellows than politics ever did," I said. "You here alone?"

"No. I have two men with me. They have worked for a long time trying to get Gambero and were willing to put in some overtime on their own."

"Where are they?"

"Farther up the beach, the hill dips in and there's a concealed spot. We've been there since this afternoon."

"Did you see the big yacht arrive?" I asked.

"Yes."

"Would you know if it's been here before?"

"It has. One of my men mentioned that he'd seen her before. Why?"

"I've got ideas about it. The crewmen carried three cases of something ashore for the Baron. He saw me watching and came over to tell me that his friends had just come back from Japan and had brought him three cases of sake. Japan is pretty close to Red China."

"Maybe you've got something," Piero said. "But we can't

get a search warrant unless we have some real evidence. Think you can find out?"

"I'm going to try," I said. "If I get a chance, I'll do it tonight, but it may not be a good time. That bunch is drinking so much they probably have to send a servant after more liquor every few minutes. If not tonight, I'll try tomorrow. If I can get out of that boar hunt, that will be a good time. If not, maybe I can get in to look at those cases after it's over. One way or another, I'll make it. You'd better try to keep an eye on the road just in case they try to take it out before I get around to it."

"I'll do it" Piero said. He thought a minute. "We'll stick around for another hour tonight. If you can get in, slip down and tell us. If not, we'll be back here tomorrow afternoon. Climb over this fence and keep on down the beach until you see us, or we see you."

"Okay," I said. "I'll make it as early as I can."

"Just one thing, Milo. The party will start breaking up around four or so, and we can't stop everyone leaving. Get down here to let us know not later than three."

"All right," I said.

"Getting anything on the Pericoloso case?" he asked.

"I'm not even trying to. I'm just pushing a little and waiting for one of them to make the first break. I've already succeeded in making the Baron dislike me."

"How?"

I told him about our conversation and he laughed. "Just the same," he said, "be careful. I don't think they'll do anything at home base, but you can never tell. Watch yourself."

"Why should I?" I said. "Blaine is watching me, Gianna

is watching me, Johnny Fornessi's watching me, Gambero's watching me, and so is young Balena. I'm the most watched man there, and they can't all be in it together."

"I wouldn't be too sure," he said. *"Buona fortuna."*

"I'll need it," I said. I turned and retraced my steps back along the beach.

When I reached the house, I turned and went along the side to where I could see the dim outlines of the wine cellar. I had just about decided to make a try at it when I saw a shadowy figure going to it from the house. When he opened the door, I could see there was a light on and another servant inside. They must have had a man on duty there during the party. I turned and went back into the house.

The show was still going on. In fact, it looked like the same act except that this girl was a blonde and was wearing roses instead of violets in the vital spots. I slipped quietly into the seat beside Gianna.

I was just in time. This had been the last act. She finally tossed the flowers into the audience and ran jiggling from the stage. The lights came on and everyone made a stampede for the room where the liquor was. Gianna and I were carried along in the crowd, although I didn't try to do anything to stop it.

"Where did you go?" Gianna asked as we got our drinks.

"I had to go to the men's room," I said.

"For so long?"

"Another March tradition," I told her. "We don't like to be rushed."

The rest of the evening went much the way it had before

dinner. Everybody got loaded and that was it—or it was until people started disappearing upstairs. I was a little loaded myself and decided I'd had enough.

"You go ahead and have fun, honey," I told Gianna. "I'm going up and go to bed."

I was expecting an argument, but she merely nodded. "All right," she said sweetly. "Good night, Milo."

I told her good night and then I hunted up a servant and told him my name and did he think he could tell me where I was sleeping. He nodded and led the way upstairs to the second floor. There it looked like a hotel. Except that there were no numbers on the doors. The servant must have operated by radar, for he went unerringly to the right door. At least it was the room where my things were. They'd been carefully hung up and put away, and I was relieved to find that my clothes were the only ones in the room. Until then I hadn't been sure.

It was quite a room. And it had its own private bath. I undressed slowly and went in and took a shower. I put on my bathrobe and came back into the room. I lit a cigarette and went over to the window. I raised it and looked out. I could just see the wine cellar. But there was no way to sneak out except to drop out the window, and I didn't feel that athletic.

I went back and sat on the edge of the bed to finish my cigarette.

"Milo," the voice came faintly from beyond the door.

I went and opened the door, looking out into the hall. There was nobody there. I closed the door and looked around.

"Milo," the voice came again.

There was another door in my room, obviously connecting with the next room. I finally realized the voice was coming from the other side of that door.

"Who is it?" I asked.

"Gianna," she said. "Please. Could you come here and help me a minute. I'm sorry."

"Sure," I said. A regular cavalier, me. I put out my cigarette in an ashtray on the dresser and opened the door.

Gianna was standing with her back to me. All she was wearing were panties and bra. Her hands were tugging at the strap of her bra.

"This damned thing is stuck," she said. "Be a dear and unfasten it for me."

I could hardly run or scream, so I advanced to the task. It unhooked so easily that it made me suspicious, but I didn't have time to voice it. The bra slipped from her shoulders as she turned around.

"Thank you, Milo," she said, smiling at me.

There comes a time when a man knows he's licked. Even if you don't like ice cream, if a cone is waved in your face long enough, there comes a time when you'll take an experimental bite. All I could do was be graceful in defeat.

But I'd been right about one thing. She was more smoke than fire and a better actress than a woman.

Later, I went back into my own room and firmly closed the door. I went in and had another shower and then smoked a cigarette while I pondered on the frailty of mankind. Then I went to bed.

I had been in bed long enough to be almost asleep before I

realized something else. There was a faint odor of perfume on my pillow. It was one I recognized. It had been on the pillow in my room in the hotel. … And the connecting door between my room and Gianna's had been open while I'd been with her.

With that thought in mind, I went to sleep, to dream that I was a Ping-Pong ball …

SIX

I was up early the following morning. Suspecting that there wouldn't be many up, I took my time about showering, shaving, and getting dressed. But it was still early when I decided to go down. The hallway was deserted and quiet. It had the feeling of a morning after. The only sound was someone snoring in the room across the hall from mine. I went on downstairs.

At least the servants were up. I was given my choice of breakfast. I decided on scrambled eggs and sausages. While they were being made, I wandered in where the bar was. It was still there, but the bartenders weren't. I rummaged around until I found the ingredients and made myself a small Bloody Mary. Then I went in and ate my breakfast with a hearty appetite.

After breakfast, I went into the barroom again. I went back and helped myself to a little very old brandy. I reminded myself that if I ever got rich I was going to have a bar like that. Just the bar and the stock, and to hell with the bartenders.

As I came out from behind the bar a flash of movement caught my eye. Someone was in the swimming pool. I walked to the terrace and looked out. It was a girl. I was just in time to see her leave the diving board and cut the water cleanly. I couldn't see who it was. I opened the doors and went out on the terrace. I reached the pool just as she came across in a fast crawl. It was Wilma Pianta.

If I'd known in advance it was she, I think I would have stayed in the house. I could still remember that scent on my pillow the night before. But now there was no retreat.

"Good morning," I said. "I didn't expect to see you—or anyone else—around yet."

"Good morning." She didn't sound any different from the way she had the night before. "I always get up early. I like the night and the early morning. I always have." There was a wistful note in her voice and I knew somehow that again she was referring back to her early life.

"You're always surprising me," I said. "I would never have guessed that you were such a good swimmer."

"I do many things well," she said simply. "You forget that I grew up in a period when one had to do things well or not live. But I didn't think you'd be up until noon. Don't all Americans sleep late?"

"Not quite," I said. "I guess I've never gotten out of the habit of getting up early either."

She had climbed out of the pool and was sitting on the edge. She pulled off her cap and her black hair tumbled down around her shoulders.

"Have you been out here often?" I asked her.

"A few times," she said.

"A strange place," I said. "Why does he throw these parties?"

"He likes parties."

"Who doesn't? But I never saw a stranger mixture of people together in my life."

"It's interesting," she said.

"That's one way of looking at it," I admitted. "Is Johnny Fornessi in business with the Baron?"

She glanced at me. "I don't know. When I am through in the office, I am through with business."

"Makes sense," I said. I lit a cigarette. "Well, I guess I'll stroll around and look this place over."

"I'll come with you," she said. She slipped her feet into a pair of sandals and stood up.

That wasn't exactly what I wanted, but I couldn't very well tell her to stay where she was. It would be like advertising that I wanted to snoop.

We walked around the back of the house. There was no one in sight. I saw to it that we walked in the direction of the wine cellar. I wouldn't get a chance to see what was in those cases, but maybe I could at least see if they were still there.

"The Baron," I said, "must have to practically buy out a distillery when he gives one of these parties."

She shrugged. "I noticed you were doing your share," she said with amusement.

"There's an old motto in my family," I said. "Never look a free drink in the cork. Or something like that. I remember that last night somebody pointed this out to me as the wine cellar and liquor storehouse. Do you suppose it's permitted to look inside?"

"I don't see why not," she said.

We walked up to the building and I swung the door open. I'd half expected it to be locked, but it wasn't. We stepped inside. It was cool there with a pleasant smell of moisture.

One side of the huge room was lined with racks in which wine bottles lay. On the other side there were shelves containing almost every kind of liquor. Over in one corner, I spotted the three cases I'd seen carried in the evening before. So at least they were still there.

"Now, if I could only back a truck up to this place," I said, "I wouldn't have any drinking problems for the rest of my life—or at least a couple of weeks."

She smiled and we went out. I'd have to try to slip back later. Now I had to go through with the pretense of wanting to see the place. I covered the same ground with Wilma that I'd covered the day before with Gianna.

We stopped beside the fence and gazed at the woods beyond. I saw some movement in the edge of the woods, but I couldn't see clearly enough to tell what animal it was.

"Baron Gambero is still living in the Middle Ages," she said. She sounded spiteful.

"You mean the boar hunting?" I asked.

"No, many people do that," she said. "But his attitude toward women."

I guessed what was in her mind. "Because he won't let women join in the hunt?" I asked.

She nodded. "I could do better than any of them."

"I'll bet you could at that," I said. I looked at her curiously. "Don't you ever feel peculiar about being a guest here?"

"What do you mean?" she asked.

"Baron Gambero," I said. "It's only a few years ago that if you or I could have found Baron Gambero, we would have killed him. He hasn't changed, but today we sit at his table and eat his food and drink his liquor."

She shrugged, looking sad for a minute. "Times have changed," she said. "It used to be that there was no doubt about who was a friend and who was an enemy. Today it is not so easy. Everybody is all mixed up with everybody else."

I nodded. I knew what she meant. It was only a few years since we had fought the great war, but already many of the lines were blurred. It was that way all over the world. When it served their purpose, Fascists and Communists and Democrats might all sit down together, or any two of them team up against the other. Cynicism was once more abroad in the land.

"Confusing, isn't it?" I said. "I try to give myself a pretty simple rule. There are certain people I dislike and ones that I like; there are ideas I dislike and ones that I like. I try to stick to those and to hell with compromising them."

She looked at me. "I like you, Milo," she said. "You know, those days just before and during the war were pretty terrible, but also they were good. One had a clearer idea of what seemed right and wrong. As you say, we knew what we liked and disliked. I like you, Milo, because you remind me of those days. Everybody else seems to have forgotten what they were really like. I have often forgotten myself. Yet everything was very real in those days. You did something because it had to be done; today we still do things, but we're not quite sure why we're doing them."

"I understand," I told her. "But what are you going to do? We'll probably keep on the way we're going until we bring those old days back. We should be able to cling to the values we learned then, without reliving them. Shall we go back to the Baron's Fascist hospitality? I will stand around and pull my forelock while he dispenses the haunches of wild boars."

She laughed without amusement and we walked back toward the house. As we neared the pool, she said, "I think I'll go in swimming again. The water is so clean and refreshing; it seems to wash all the stains away. Why don't you get a suit and come in, too?"

"No, thanks," I said. "I've taken a vow to never swim in anything deeper than a brandy and soda. That's my own personal form of giving up."

She had put on her bathing cap, tucking her black hair in under the edges. "Each to his own," she said and dived into the water. I watched her knife her way across the pool and then turned back to the house. It was immediately evident that other guests were up and about. I went inside.

Almost everyone looked as if he'd had a rough night—which was true. There seemed no chance for me to go snooping again immediately, so I made myself useful by introducing most of the guests to a Bloody Mary. There's nothing like it for that morning-after feeling, and I soon won the undying gratitude of dozens of guests.

They kept straggling downstairs by twos and fours and having breakfast. The combination of food and liquor restored most of them, and it wasn't long before there were a number of girls in the pool with Wilma. I was wondering why the men didn't go in when I realized that the Baron was already getting everything organized for the boar hunt.

I tried to evade this, but when that wasn't possible, I tried to beg off on the grounds that I had no hunting clothes with me.

But everyone seemed determined that not a single man was going to miss the hunt. I had a secret suspicion that this was a simple case of misery loving company. Whatever it was, I was soon outfitted with the proper clothes. I felt pretty silly about the whole thing. I went into my room and changed. Enough of my old habits stuck with me so that I put my shoulder holster on beneath the hunting coat. Maybe they were going to give me a high-powered rifle, but I felt safer with a gun nestling beneath my arm.

"Tallyho and yoicks," I said to myself in the mirror. Then I went downstairs and managed to sneak two more fast drinks before all of us—looking like a cartoon in *Punch*—marched solemnly from the house and down to the gun house.

We got into the gun house and everyone started picking out his gun. Everyone but me. I stood looking at the damn things and having no idea of what to pick. I didn't know what one used to shoot a wild pig and I didn't much care. The Baron must have noticed my predicament.

"Riccardo," he shouted, "help our good friend, Signor March, pick out a gun."

Young Balena came over. He didn't look especially happy at the idea of helping me; he probably would rather have used a gun on me than to show me how to use one. But he was obviously determined to make the best of a bad show.

"Ever hunted boars before?" he asked me.

"No," I said. I refrained from adding that it was all right with me if we dropped the whole thing right there.

"The woods are pretty thick," he said. "Lots of thorns and undergrowth, which means that most of the shots are at close range. Something like this is probably best." He reached out and pulled a gun from the racks. "This is a .375 Weatherby. A good gun."

"Anything like a .22?" I asked.

He wasn't amused. "This will stop a charging pig, which is the chief idea," he said. He reached to a shelf above the racks and pulled down a box of shells. He quickly loaded the gun, working the action to be sure it was all right. He handed the rest of the shells to me. "The gun is fully loaded now," he said. "All you have to do is pull the trigger."

"That sounds easy," I said, trying to be helpful.

"Just remember," he said, "that you won't be able to see very far once we're in where the pigs are. That doesn't apply only to the pigs. If you're careless with a gun, it's pretty easy to shoot a man without even seeing him."

"Let's hope the memory of that is completely mutual," I told him. "I don't mind being called a pig, but I'd hate to be shot like one. I want at least a chance to grunt once."

He didn't bother to answer. He turned away and started picking out a gun for himself.

Finally everyone had a gun and we left the building. We walked down to the fence. The gate was already open and about a dozen servants in rough clothing were through and heading for the woods.

"What's with them?" I asked of nobody in particular.

"Beaters," Baron Gambero said. "They're going in ahead of us to stir up the boars so we can get shots at them. Otherwise they're apt to sleep all day."

"I didn't realize they were that smart," I said.

"Another thing, Signor March," the Baron said. "You will be able to recognize the boars by their tusks. There are a lot of sows in the woods, too, but they will leave you alone and I would prefer that they are not shot. We like to kill only the boars. And they are dangerous. When you see a boar coming for you, do not lose any time in shooting."

"Don't worry," I told him. "I have no desire to be served, with an apple in my mouth, for a wild boar's dinner. That would be carrying justice too far."

We went through the gate and it was closed behind us. We walked in a group down to the edge of the woods. Then we began splitting up into small groups, each fanning off by itself.

"Signor March," Baron Gambero said, "since this is your first hunt, I suggest that you stay with Riccardo and myself. We are more experienced and it will be better."

I could think of a lot of people I would rather be with, but I didn't say anything. It turned out that there would be three other men with us, and somehow that made me feel better. The six of us headed directly into the woods.

We had gone perhaps a hundred yards when the woods began to thicken up and we began to run into patches of thorns. The six of us fanned out as we went. Two of the men were on my right, with Gambero, Riccardo, and the other man on my left. Far ahead of us I could hear the beaters setting up a racket.

Soon we were deep in the thickets. I could hear the other men, but I could no longer see them. Thorns tore at my jacket and pants, and I began to be grateful for the heavy clothes they'd given me. The thorns had finally become almost a solid wall. I cast around trying to find an opening and finally discovered a trail of sorts through which I could go with only minor wounds. The trail zigzagged so that I could only see fifteen or twenty feet ahead of me, and I could see nothing on either side. It didn't impress me as the proper place to meet an angry boar, and I was hoping that the boars would have more sense than we did about this thing.

The shouting ahead of me had increased in intensity and suddenly a gun went off with a crash.

"I missed him," a voice shouted, followed by a few choice curses.

"He's slipped in between us," another voice shouted.

Everybody was sounding pretty excited, and I was wishing I could just see someone. I could feel the tension knotting my muscles as I tried to guess what was going on.

"Signor March," another voice shouted. I recognized it as the Baron's. "Where are you?"

"Here," I yelled.

"I think he is heading your way. Be on the watch."

He was wasting his breath. I was already on the watch. By this time I could hear a crashing of the thorns and a loud grunting noise somewhere ahead. But I couldn't see anything. I half lifted the rifle and stood still. I could feel my heart thudding. Right then I would have appreciated the feeling of Madison Avenue under my feet.

Suddenly the boar came into view, straight ahead of me and not very far away. He was huge, twice as big as I had imagined one might be. I had a brief glimpse of mud-encrusted bristles, tiny wrinkled eyes, and long curved tusks. He was charging straight down the path toward me with what seemed the speed of a locomotive. And there was no room to step to one side even if I wanted to be polite. Which I did.

I brought the rifle up automatically, and when the sights were lined up on his head, I pulled the trigger. Nothing happened.

It was probably no more than a second that I stood there, absorbing the shock of the gun's not working, but it seemed like an hour. There was a prickly sensation in my scalp as though I were feeling my hair turn gray. I realized that the gun must have jammed, but my thoughts didn't go beyond that. My first feeling was to turn and run, even though the same feeling encompassed the awareness that it was useless. But then instinct took over.

I dropped the rifle. In the same movement, my right hand reached for the gun in my shoulder holster and I dropped down on one knee. The boar was so close I could almost count the bristles on his head.

I lifted the gun and steadied it, aiming for the boar's right eye. I pulled the trigger and there was something comforting in the feel of the gun bucking against the palm of my hand. I pulled the trigger again. With the second shot, I saw the boar's eye vanish. I pulled the trigger again and again. The shots were loud and the gun powder bit into my nostrils.

The boar's front legs buckled, folding slowly at the knees. Then his head was down, the tusks plowing up the ground and throwing dirt on me. I stayed on the one knee, almost hypnotized, and watched him sliding toward me. When he finally came to a stop, one tusk was less than six inches from my knee. Blood was trickling from the spot where his eye had been. His back legs twitched a few times and then the last fight went out of his muscles. A strong odor of musk mixed with the smell of gunpowder.

I could hear the other men shouting to me, but their voices seemed to come from a great distance and were not very important.

As soon as I realized the boar was really dead, I sat down on the ground and the reaction set in. My hands were shaking so badly I could hardly get the gun back in its holster. With considerable difficulty I got a cigarette out and lit it with the third match.

I heard the voices drawing nearer, but I did nothing to help them locate me. I sat on the ground and shook—and thought. I was remembering that it had been young Balena who had loaded the gun and given it to me. I remembered his trying the action and assuring me that it was all right. I couldn't prove it, but I was willing to bet that he had jammed the gun right then.

If it hadn't been for the fact that I'd gotten annoyed at Johnny Fornessi and borrowed a gun from Piero, I would now have been dead and nobody in the world could have proved it wasn't an accident.

I was still sitting there, and still shaking, when Gambero, young Balena, and one of the other men came into sight along the trail. They stopped and stared when they saw me.

"Are you all right, Signore?" the third man asked anxiously.

"Sure," I said. "I always sit down with the boar's head in my lap after I've killed one."

"What happened?" Baron Gambero asked. "That didn't sound like your gun being fired."

"It wasn't," I said. "The gun jammed."

The Baron walked over and picked up the gun and looked at it. "Strange," he said. "This is a gun that seldom jams."

"It wasn't easy," I told him. "Everything I am or have I owe to my friends."

Did I imagine it, or did he and Riccardo exchange glances?

"But how did you kill the boar?" the third man asked.

"With this," I said. I pulled the gun from its holster.

"Small arms on a boar hunt?" the man said. "I never heard of it—but it was lucky you had it, Signore."

"You surprise me, Signor March," Baron Gambero said. "I thought you said you used only your brains in your hunting."

"I do," I said. "That's why I had this along. By the way, it's even more effective on smaller game." I looked at Riccardo and put the gun away.

The third man was walking around the boar. "This is a big one," he said. "It must run well over four hundred pounds."

"I could've sworn it weighed four thousand pounds when it was charging me," I said. I stood up and was relieved to find that my knees had stopped shaking.

"I think we can fix the gun," the Baron said, "and then we can go on with the hunt."

"No, thanks," I said. "I want to keep it the way it is, as a souvenir." I reached out and took the gun from his hands.

"You mean," the third man said in amazement, "that you will continue to hunt with the small gun?"

"No," I said. "I once promised my old mother that I would never kill more than one boar in a day. I've had it. I'm going back to the house and hunt for a drink. I don't think I'll need a gun for that."

Without waiting to see what they thought about it, I turned and headed back the way I'd come. It wasn't until I was out of the woods and nearing the fence that it occurred to me that I might have encountered a boar on the way back and have needed the gun. The boar wouldn't have had any way of knowing that I was throwing in the sponge.

I left the gun leaning against the door of the gun house and went on up to the main house. I headed straight for the bar. A bartender was once more in evidence. I decided my case called for strong measures so I had him mix me a double, extra dry martini.

After two of them, the tremor was gone from my fingers. I took a third and went upstairs to my room. I stripped off my clothes and went in and had a shower. When I came out, I sat naked and finished my drink and a cigarette. I was beginning to feel more normal—and more convinced that Riccardo Balena had tried to kill me. But I couldn't really complain about that. Everything I'd done had been calculated to push them into action—and now it had started.

I got dressed. I reloaded the gun and strapped it on again. Then I went downstairs. I collected another drink and went out on the terrace. All the women were there, in the pool, or on the tennis courts.

Looking around, I soon located Gianna. She was at the pool in a scarlet bathing suit that must have been made by someone who was afraid of using too much material. I went over to her.

"Back so soon?" she said. "Where are the others?"

"I've been back for some time," I said. "You know me; I hate to be late. I thought you might be missing me."

"I was," she said seriously. "How did you do?"

"Great," I said. "I shot one boar, but he looked at me so sadly—the way my grandmother used to look when Grandfather kicked her—I didn't have the heart to kill another one."

"Oh, you," she said. It was her favorite expression. "Oh, here come the others now."

She was right. Home were the hunters. They were straggling up toward the house, all of them looking very manly and pleased with themselves. The servants were with them, carrying six large, and very dead, hogs. It made quite a procession.

I was aware of the time slipping away. I'd thought that I might get down to look in the cases before the others returned, but I had killed too much time. I'd have to try to make it while the others were dressing, or shortly thereafter.

Even as the guests were streaming into the house, the servants were going to work on the boars. They had quickly rigged up poles and were hanging the boars by their feet. When they were all hung, one of the men departed for the main house at a trot. The others immediately went to work, gutting the boars. I noticed that others were already carrying big pots of boiling water down to where they were working on the pigs.

The gutting was already done. Some of the servants had

pulled down two of the boars and were taking them toward the huge freezer. Others were dousing the remaining hogs with the hot water and starting to scrape the bristles off. I was so fascinated watching them that I did not hear Baron Gambero approaching.

"Signor March," he said loudly. I looked around to see him standing directly behind us. He was still wearing his hunting clothes. "I have the honor to announce that you have won the prize for the largest boar killed in today's hunt. Your boar weighed four hundred and eighty-six pounds."

"Well, goody for me," I said in English. I realized that this was hardly adequate and I switched back to Italian. "It was really nothing," I said. "You might even say that the boar picked me rather than the other way around; perhaps we should give the prize to the boar."

Several of the women giggled and the Baron frowned. I realized I hadn't helped the situation any.

"I'm really honored," I added. Then, mostly to change the subject, I gestured toward where some of his men were carrying the two boars into the freezer. "What's happening down there, Baron? Why are they butchering four of the hogs and not the other two?"

He brightened up. "The two that are being taken into the freezer," he said, "are for the Sisters of Gentle Mercy in Tuscany. It is a convent which was started by an ancestor of mine. Two boars from every hunt go to them; it is a pledge of mine. They are frozen whole and then delivered to the convent. The others are being butchered for the servants."

"I imagine they must be very grateful," I said.

He missed the sarcasm in my voice. He nodded. "They are," he said. His tone announced that that was the way it should be. "Now, if you will excuse me ..." He left without waiting to see if I would excuse him.

"Oh, Milo," Gianna said, "you did kill the largest boar. I'm so proud of you."

"Did you ever stop to think how the boar might feel about it?" I asked her. "He was probably mortified at being killed by a mere American. After all, the nearest my ancestors ever came to wild boar hunting was trapping a mouse in the kitchen. Think what the sows must be saying to each other now."

"What are they saying?"

"Oink," I said.

"Oh, Milo," she said. "You are making the joke again."

"Am I?" I said in mock surprise. "I thought I was just grunting." As soon as I said it, I was sorry. It wasn't Gianna's fault that all of her assets were below her shoulders. The Baron was fair game, but I had no right to make fun of her.

"I'm sorry, Gianna. I'm in a foul mood and I'm taking most of it out on you. That's not fair."

"It's all right, Milo," she said. The way she said it made me feel more ashamed of myself. "I don't understand you most of the time, but whatever you do is all right."

That made me feel even worse—partly because I wasn't giving her my full attention. I was too busy watching what was happening on the other side of the house. The two hogs had been put into the freezer and now the servants were busy butchering the other four. But something new had been added. Another servant had appeared from the main house. He looked like the butler, although I wasn't sure. He had walked stolidly down to the wine cellar and was now on his way toward the freezer. He was carrying something, but I couldn't see what it was.

"You're a very sweet girl, Gianna," I said with the half of my attention I was giving her. For the minute I was tempted to tell her that she was wasting her time, that the only way I could ever get her to Hollywood would be to buy her a ticket, but I knew it would only mess things up. "I shall remember you in my will."

"You're not *that* old," she said.

Just the way she said it hardened my resolve. I wasn't even that old. "Oh, I don't know," I said. "This time I got the prize. The next time somebody may get the prize for bringing me down. Did you ever think of that?"

The butler, if that's who it was, had left the freezer and was going back to the wine cellar.

"I thought I might get the prize for that," she said, proving that she wasn't as dumb as she looked. I glanced at her and decided that with the bathing suit she was wearing, it didn't make any difference if she were.

"Honey," I told her gently, "for that you don't get a prize; you get sent back two grades for doing something that's too easy."

"Non capisco," she said.

"Another joke," I said, reaching out to pat her shoulder. "And not a very good one. Forget it, honey."

The butler had come out of the wine cellar and was going back to the freezer.

"All right, Milo," she said submissively.

I patted her shoulder again and watched the butler. I was getting more and more interested—and getting an idea.

We continued to chatter, while I watched the butler make several more trips between the wine cellar and the freezer. Finally, he made what was apparently his last trip and headed back for the house. The other servants were still busily butchering on the far side of the freezer.

I glanced into the house. There was no one in sight except the bartender, so apparently all the men were still busy changing clothes.

I became aware that Gianna had said something. "I'm sorry," I told her. "What did you say?"

"Just that I'd better go in and change," she said. "Everyone else is going."

I looked around and realized that the pool was almost deserted.

"Within the hour," Gianna said, "many will start going home and we probably should before it's too late."

"That's a good idea, honey," I said. "You go ahead and change. I'll wait here for you."

"I won't be long," she said. She stood up and walked away. Normally, her walk was something to watch, especially in that bathing suit, but now I didn't even glance at her. It looked as if this was my chance to check up, and I didn't have long before I had to be down on the beach to meet Piero.

It wasn't much except a hunch, but I felt certain that the butler had been moving the contents of those three cases from the wine cellar to the freezer. If I was right, that only seemed to clinch it. Certainly no one would move any sort of alcoholic drink into a freezer.

I got up and walked around the back of the house. I could reach the freezer without being seen by the servants who were butchering. No one else was in sight. My only danger was in being spotted from the main house. I'd have to depend on luck from that quarter.

I sauntered slowly across the lawn, stopping to show interest in some flower beds and also stopping for a brief look at the wine cellar. By easy stages, I made it on to the freezer. I acted as if I were going by and then, as an afterthought, had decided to take a look at it. I turned back and opened the door. Without seeming to, I took a quick look around. There was nobody in sight. I slipped inside and closed the door.

The freezer was cold. I started shivering almost the minute I was in it. The two wild boars were hanging from hooks in the middle of the room. Everything made me feel that they were the focal points. I went over to one of them and stuck my hand into the gaping belly wound.

It was almost too easy. Immediately my hand struck a package. I brought it out and unwrapped it. I was staring at a brown, gum-like mess. I lifted it to my face and sniffed. It had a sour, earthy smell, something like rotten potatoes. Just to make sure, I squeezed off a small part of it and popped it into my mouth. It tasted bitter. I spat it out. There was no question about it. This was raw opium.

I rewrapped the package and put it back inside the carcass of the hog. I went to the door and opened it, peering outside. There was no one in sight. I was halfway to the house when I thought of something. There was a chance that someone had seen me and they would try to move the opium while I was down contacting Piero. I should have taken one package out and hidden it somewhere else so that there would be some evidence for the detectives to find.

It was such a good idea that I decided to go back and do it. There was still no one about and I felt confident that I could do it. I turned and walked slowly and casually back toward the freezer.

I had almost reached it when I thought I heard a noise behind me, a hurried yet furtive sound. I started to turn.

My head suddenly exploded with pain. It was sharp and intense, the pain that brings with it a sudden white light in the back of the eyes—and then blackness. I felt myself falling, but the darkness wiped even that out. And then there was nothing.

I came back to consciousness slowly. I was first aware of a sound—the steady, rhythmic murmur you hear in a sea shell. I shook my head, trying to shake some sense into it. Slowly I became aware that the sound was voices. The next thing that came to my senses was my head. It hurt. It hurt like hell, with a pounding that threatened to drown out even the murmur of voices.

Next I realized that somebody was holding my head. My only complaint was that it wasn't being held gently enough. My head was a delicate thing at the moment. I didn't want anyone messing around with it.

I was afraid to open my eyes. In some way, I felt that my eyelids were fastened to the spot that hurt and it would be worse if I opened them.

"Milo, my friend," a voice said in Italian, "you must wake up. Please. For the love of the Virgin Mother ..."

That did it. No character was going to talk to me like that while he thought I was unconscious. I opened my eyes with an effort. I was surprised to find it still light, the sun blazing down. I resented it. The way my head was hurting, I should have been out until at least midnight.

It hurt to move my eyeballs, but I rolled my eyes up to see who was holding my head. I wanted to see who was giving me all that jazz. I got another surprise. It was Piero.

"No sonuvabitch is going to talk to me like that while he thinks I'm unconscious," I said. "Where did you come from, Piero?"

"Milo," he exclaimed, "you are alive. You are talking. You have come back from the dead."

"Who's dead?" I demanded indignantly. "There's nothing wrong with me."

"Good," he said. "Who hit you?"

"I'm dying," I said, "and he wants to know who hit me. How the hell do I know who hit me? He came up behind me." I had looked around enough to see that there were a lot of people standing not too far away. I lowered my voice. "Where'd you come from, Piero?"

He looked at me sadly. "You were supposed to come to the beach before three o'clock. You didn't come and already some of the guests were leaving. I came up to see why and found you here."

"You found me?"

"Yes. No one else had looked around here. At least, they said that no one knew you were here."

"Somebody knew," I said bitterly. "I didn't hit myself."

"Who hit you?" he asked again. "Was it him?"

"Who's him?" I asked, twisting my head to look in the direction Piero was indicating. Then I saw him. Riccardo Balena was lying on the ground not far from me. He was lying on his back, staring at the sky with unseeing eyes. His throat had been cut, and it gaped like a huge lipsticked mouth.

"I don't know," I said. "But I didn't do that to him."

"Of course you didn't," he said. "You couldn't have cut a deck of cards, my friend. You were lucky your head wasn't crushed."

Memory was coming back to me. "Piero," I said, "where are your two men?"

"They are here. Why?"

"Send one of them into the freezer—that building there. There are two wild boars hanging from the ceiling. Inside them are packages of raw opium—lots of it. At least, they were there before I was knocked out."

He called one of his men and gave him the order in a low voice. The man went over to the freezer and swung open the door. Out of the corner of my eye I saw one figure start to drift away from the crowd. I realized that it was Baron Gambero. But Piero had seen him, too.

"Fermi quell'uomo," he snapped.

By twisting my head, I was able to see another man step forward quickly and stop the Baron.

"Good boy," I said.

The first detective came out of the freezer and he had a package in his hand. He nodded to Piero.

"Milo, I love you like a brother," Piero said fervently. "I forgive you for everything. I forgive you for the blonde, I forgive you for the cemetery, I forgive you for the long wait on the beach."

"You forgive me," I said. I was so annoyed that I forgot my headache and sat up. "I'm the guy who had to face a charging wild boar; I'm the guy who got hit over the head and *you* forgive *me?"*

"But you are an American," he said gravely. "Americans like that sort of thing. How is your head?"

"It's terrible," I said. Now that he'd reminded me, it was. "You see that building over there? Tell your man to go in it and bring me a bottle of very old brandy. That's the only thing that will make it better."

He gave the detective an order and he went. In a moment he was back with a bottle of brandy. It was very old. I took a long drink of it and immediately felt better.

"Now let's get organized," I said.

"First," Piero said, "you should know all that's happened."

"I was hit on the head," I said indignantly. "What else happened?"

"When we got here," he said, "we found you on this very spot unconscious. Young Balena was where he is still lying. Up at the corner of the house, we found Gianna Bionda."

"What happened to her?" I asked.

"She claims that she was on the terrace when she heard some sort of noise from this direction. She started to come around the house and that's all she knows. There was a knife in her shoulder. It must have been thrown."

"By whom?" I asked.

"Balena's throat was cut and Gianna had a knife in her shoulder," he said. "You were unconscious. But guess who we discovered hiding by the cars?"

I turned to look in the direction he was indicating. Achille Coniglio was standing there, looking sulky.

"He had one knife on him," Piero added.

"I didn't do it," Achille said sullenly, looking at me. "I came here because you said you were going to look for the killer of my brother and I thought perhaps you would need me. But I did not even know you were in danger, Milo."

I turned to look. It was impossible to see the places where the cars are parked.

"I believe you, Achille," I said. "You must not pay any attention to the police. They get excited."

"Look who doesn't get excited," Piero said.

"I do not get excited," I said with dignity. "I may get hit on the head, but I do not get excited. By the way, the butler is in on this little deal here."

Piero snapped an order and one of the detectives went toward the house.

"If you're interested," I said, "the opium was brought in by the big yacht. Three men and a woman."

"It's left," he said, "but we can get them."

"The way it worked," I said, "was like this: They'd bring the opium in when he was having a party. Nobody paid any attention to four more guests. Always there would be a boar hunt. The Baron has a tradition of sending two boars from each hunt to a convent in Tuscany. I don't know if he really did, but the opium always left here hidden inside the boars. That's all there was to it."

"Good," Piero said. "Now all you have to do is to tell me who hit you, murdered young Balena, and knifed Gianna."

I'd been thinking about it even while I talked, and I didn't like what I was thinking. But I kept coming back to it.

"Another thing," I said, lowering my voice. "Riccardo here tried to kill me this afternoon when we were on the boar hunt. I expect he was the lad who hit me over the head. And I'm sure there is no question that he was mixed in on this deal with Gambero."

Piero looked worried.

"I know what you're thinking," I said. "The government. All right. I agree. It's important to keep the government you have. The boy's father is not automatically tainted with the son's sins. So make up your own story. You can say that Riccardo rushed in to save me when I was attacked. So he'll be a hero and so will his father."

"Killed by whom?" Piero asked quietly.

"In good time," I said irritably. "You want strawberries *and* whipped cream. But won't that save your government?"

"Yes," he said. "You'll back up such a story?"

"Yeah," I said. "If he were alive, I wouldn't. But you can't send him to prison now. And the only person who can say otherwise is Gambero, and who's going to believe him?" I suddenly remembered something. "You said some of the guests had already left. Who?"

He told me. It had been quite a few of them. The only ones I knew were the four from the yacht, Johnny Fornessi and

Wilma Pianta, Ugo Marrone and Albert Blaine.

"Okay," I said. I stood up and managed not to fall on my face. My head felt better, but I was very tired. I didn't think it was all due to the blow on the head. "Your two men can take in Gambero and the butler and the evidence, can't they?"

"Yes."

"Let's go to Rome. I wasn't cut out for this country life."

Piero was willing, but it still took us a few minutes to get started. Gianna, with a bandage on her shoulder, insisted on being taken along. We finally wound up taking her car, with Piero driving. At my insistence, we also took Achille along.

Piero only made one more reference to the matter at hand. That was just before we got into the car.

"Milo, my friend," he said, "you have not forgotten about the murderer?"

"How the hell could I forget?" I asked. I laughed, but I wasn't amused. "You know something, Piero? The murderer has killed at least one hundred ninety-three people—one hundred ninety-six counting Anna Maria Pericoloso and Attilio Coniglio and Riccardo Balena. But I owe my life to the murderer, and you owe your narcotics case against Gambero to the murderer. And you want to know why? Because some damn fool colonel in the United States Army decided years ago to put a parachute on a character named Milo March and boot him out of an airplane. You want to know what else?"

"What else, Milo?" he asked gently.

"It's a stinking world," I said. I took another pull from the brandy bottle that I was still carrying and then climbed into the car. We started back for Rome.

For once Gianna was feeling too bad to chatter, and I was just as glad. She sat in the front with Piero and I sat in the back with Achille. I could tell that he was dying to talk to me about the thing nearest to his heart, but he wouldn't start it without some sign from me.

"Later, Achille," I told him and he nodded. There was a trusting look in his eyes, and I felt lousy about him, too.

None of us talked for the rest of the trip. I sat in the back and nipped on the bottle and thought my dark, secret thoughts.

It was shortly after five o'clock when we arrived back in Rome. Piero was like another part of myself. Without asking, he first dropped Gianna at a hospital and explained to her that we would return her car to her later in the evening. She was still so upset, she did nothing but give us a pale smile and trot obediently up the steps of the hospital. Piero swung the car around and drove straight to the street where Achille lived.

"I will come to see you soon, Achille," I said as the boy got out of the car. "Maybe tonight, maybe in the morning."

"All right, Milo," he said. *"Buona notte."*

"Buona notte," I called as Piero sent the little car darting away from the sidewalk. As soon as we reached a place where there were public phones, he pulled to the curb.

"I must call in," he said, "and make a report. Then I will be at your service, my friend."

"I have to make a call, too," I said.

I left the brandy in the car and we both went inside. He took one phone and I took another one at some distance from him. My call didn't take long, just enough time to get an address. Then I went out to the car and waited.

After a few minutes, Piero came out and got behind the wheel. "Everything is in motion," he said. "There will not be much sleep in the Interior building tonight, I can tell you. But the news will be good to many people."

"Including the man from the American Embassy," I said. "I should call him, but it won't hurt him to have one more night of troubled sleep. It'll keep him on his toes."

"I have told them there are still some loose ends," Piero said, "and that I will report in later. Where to, Milo?"

I gave him the address. "I think," I added.

We drove across Rome without talking. When Piero finally found the address, I was surprised to see that it was a very modern apartment house. I suppose I shouldn't have been surprised.

Piero turned off the motor and looked at me. I think from his expression he had already guessed. "You want me to go up?" he asked quietly.

"I suppose you should," I said. "I have no authority in Rome, but I think it might be better if I did it."

"I understand," he said. I remembered then that he'd had the same experience and that he probably did understand. "I will wait here for you, Milo."

I nodded and took a drink from the bottle. I wiped the top of my sleeve and offered it. "I remember we used to drink this way," I said, "even though the contents weren't always this old or mellow. Will you have a drink on the house, Piero?"

He took the bottle and drank from it. Then he, too, wiped it on his sleeve and handed it back. I took the bottle and got out of the car.

"I'll be back soon," I said.

"Take your time," he said. He'd leaned back in the seat and lighted a cigarette. "What is it you Americans say? Rome wasn't built in a day?"

"Or rebuilt," I told him. I turned and went into the apartment building. I found the name and pressed the button beneath it Almost immediately the buzzer sounded for me to come up. I had thought it would be that way.

I had noticed the number beside the name. I went up to the third floor and along the hall until I came to the door. I pressed the button beside it.

The door opened and Wilma Pianta was smiling at me. "Hello, Milo," she said. Her voice was soft and feminine. "Come in." She stood to one side as I entered. "You are the first person to enter here besides myself," she said.

I looked around the room and I could see why. All four walls of the room were literally covered with knives. There was every kind imaginable, from a tiny two-inch dagger to a giant thing that was almost a sword. They were all arranged to make decorative patterns, and in a way it was beautiful. In another way, it made the muscles of my stomach contract.

"I brought some brandy," I said. I offered her the bottle.

She looked at me and understood the way I meant it. She took the bottle and tilted it to her lips. She wiped the mouth of the bottle on the skirt of her sleeveless dress and handed it back. I took a drink.

"This one," she said, pointing to an old, stained knife on one of the walls, "is the one I used years ago."

"La Ragazza," I said.

She nodded. "It drank a lot of Fascist blood." She looked pleased for a minute, then her face fell into almost childish lines. "What happened to us, Milo?"

"To the world," I said gently. "It was bathed in blood, Wilma. I'm not sure that anyone ever got over it, or ever will."

She nodded again. "I am very good with a knife; it was the one thing I learned better than all other things." She looked at me. "Riccardo was going to kill you."

"I guessed that," I said. "And you could have done better with Gianna if you had wanted to."

"Yes. I was going to kill her, but then I thought maybe you liked her."

"No more nor less than anyone else, but I'm glad you didn't kill her." I took another drink from the bottle and passed it to her.

"It was terrible after the war," she said as though she knew the question in my mind. "Suddenly I was nobody and I had nothing to do. I tried to work, but that was no good. I couldn't sleep at nights. For a while, I thought the answer was men—a lot of men, but that was no good either. When I found it out, I never had another man until you. Except for one of the old men. I felt sorry for him." She was looking to see if I believed her and I nodded. "But I worked at jobs because I had to live," she said. "And I would come home at night and play with the knives. It was the only time I felt alive. Then two years ago, I got the job with Signor Manzo. At about the same time, I met Johnny Fornessi. I did not fall in love with him, or even like him, yet I found it exciting to be around him. There was something about him that made me feel alive."

"A sense of violence," I suggested.

"Perhaps," she said with a shrug. "I didn't stop to think. And he seemed to know a lot that I was thinking and feeling. When he suggested that we ... work together, I found the idea attractive. And then suddenly I was living again, it was almost like the old days. Can you understand that, Milo?"

I nodded.

"I thought you could," she said. "The other day, in your room, I thought perhaps it was over. And this afternoon, I knew you would come for me—that was why I made Johnny drive me back here immediately—and in a way I was glad."

I understood that, too. I think I understood the whole thing very well. Her world had trained her to kill and had made her a perfect machine at it. Then it had suddenly told her to stop, but that was the only thing she knew. She'd had to start again, but it hadn't been the same thing, and she hadn't been happy at it. She had been destined never to be happy again the day that her function was no longer needed. And probably that day something had snapped inside her.

"Johnny Fornessi gave you part of the money?" I asked.

"Yes," she said, "but it's all in the bank. I never spent any of it."

"What about Anna Maria Pericoloso?" I asked gently.

"We were at the Baron's," she said. "Johnny came over and told me that it had to be done, and that it must look like an accident. He said that the girl knew things about them all and was going to tell the police because Riccardo no longer loved her. She was asleep in her room—I think she had been drugged—and I did not hurt her at all. Later, Johnny and the Baron and Riccardo took her down to the beach."

"Which knife did you use on her?" I asked.

"That one," she said, pointing to a dagger with a long, needle-like blade. "It was the one I used on most of them—but I never hurt any of them."

"I know," I said gently. "I think we'd better go, Wilma."

"Johnny didn't know about this afternoon," she said with a little smile. "Milo, couldn't we stay here tonight and go in the morning?"

"I don't think so," I said. "A friend of mine is waiting downstairs."

She nodded and looked at me. Her gaze was that of a child. "Will they kill me, Milo?"

"No," I told her. "I am certain they will not kill you, Wilma. I will not let them."

"I know you won't," she said. She went into the next room and came out with a light coat. "I am ready, Milo."

We went out and walked down the two flights of stairs. As we reached the door, she took my hand. I returned the pressure of her fingers. We walked outside and got into the car. She smiled at Piero as he started the motor.

We drove back to the Ministry of the Interior without talking. I had my arm around Wilma and she leaned her head on my shoulder. We went inside and turned Wilma over to a matron. I leaned over and kissed her on the cheek before she was led away.

I told Piero about Johnny Fornessi and the money in the bank and the knives on the wall, including the needle-pointed dagger which could be fitted to wounds. Then I left, telling him that I would be waiting for him in the bar of my hotel.

I took a taxi back to the hotel and went into the bar, I told the bartender to make me a double martini.

I was on my second one when the redhead came and sat on the stool next to mine.

She looked to be maybe thirty, or a little more. She was very beautiful.

"You are an American, are you not?" she asked with a little smile.

"Yes," I said.

"I knew an American once," she said. "It was during the war."

I was in no mood for it. "The last war or the next one?" I asked her.

The smile froze on her face and she slid from the stool.

She moved down the bar and sat next to a man who obviously talked more sanely.

After a while Piero came. That night we both got very drunk.

SEVEN

When I awakened the next morning I was alone. And I had a double headache. The front part hurt from the drinking the night before, and the back part hurt from the blow. I felt drained, and that wasn't from either thing.

I called downstairs and ordered a double Bloody Mary and a pot of coffee. I went in and took a cold shower while I was waiting for it. I came out and had the drink. By the time I started on the coffee, I felt better.

I checked my watch. It was four o'clock in the morning in New York, but I didn't care. I put through a call to Martin Raymond at his home.

When he answered, I let him splutter about the time long enough to be completely awake. Then I told him the news. He stopped spluttering and he didn't even care what time it was. I talked to him for another few minutes and then hung up.

After that I called Luigi Manzo at the Rome office. He was spluttering too, but I cut him short and told him what I had in mind. Then I told him that I wouldn't see him again right away and hung up while he was still thanking me. I called the airport and got a reservation on the next plane. It would be leaving in about two hours. Then I called Piero.

"How are you?" I asked him.

He groaned. "I am all head and no brains," he said. "Fortunately there is little to do today. There are now only details, and others can do those just as well. Incidentally, I don't think Signorina Pianta will even go to trial. She has been examined, and the recommendation is that she be sent to an institution."

"Good," I said. "Come and drive me somewhere."

"I will be right there," he said.

I hung up and packed my clothes. Then I went downstairs and checked out, arranging for my luggage to be sent to the airport. I waited in the lobby for Piero.

"Signor March," the clerk called over to me while I was waiting, "there is a Signor Blaine on the phone from the American Embassy. He wishes to talk to you."

"Tell him I'll send him a postcard from New York," I said.

In a few minutes I saw Piero drive up in front of the hotel. I went out and got into the car beside him. He grinned at me.

"Have you seen the papers?" he asked.

"No," I said. I had deliberately not looked at any of them.

"There's one there on the back seat. Take a look."

I twisted around and looked at the paper. There were several headlines. One said: *Son of Minister of the Interior Dies a Hero.* Another announced the arrest of Baron Gambero. The third said: *Detective Breaks Up Murder and Drug Ring with Aid of American.*

"It's a little wrong," Piero said, "but I thought you ought to have some of the credit."

"Big of you," I grunted. "Remind me not to put you on the expense account the next time."

I told him to take me down to see Achille. Within a half hour he was parking across the street from the wineshop.

"I'll be back in a minute," I said. "By the way, did you get Johnny Fornessi?"

"We got him. And I'm sure the insurance ring business will take care of him."

"Good," I said. I crossed the street and went up the stairs. I walked back to the last door and knocked.

"Avanti," the voice said.

I opened the door and walked in. Achille sat on his bed, honing that knife again.

"You came," he said.

"I told you I would," I said. "The killer of your brother is caught."

He looked disappointed. "You did not let me get to him."

"It was not a him, but a her. She was very sick in the head, Achille, and she is being sent away. She killed your brother because a man told her to, and that man will go to prison. It is better this way."

"If you say so," he said.

"I have come to offer you a trade," I said.

"What is it?"

"The chance to become a man who sells information on even a bigger scale than your brother did."

"How is that?"

"In a way that is what I do," I said. "I came here working for an American insurance company. They will soon need someone here in Rome who will collect information and sell it only to them. You can be that man. You will go to work for them now and learn about the business. Then in about a year you can be trained for the job of getting information. Perhaps I will even come over and train you myself."

"Truly?"

"Truly. And you will be paid money every week even while you are training. Do you think you might like that?"

"It is wonderful," he said. He grew thoughtful. "But you mentioned a trade. What is it you want from me for this?"

"The knife," I said, holding out my hand. "You will not need it in this job. You will learn to use your brains, which are much sharper than any knife."

He hesitated a minute, then he reached out and placed the knife in my hand.

"If you say so," he said.

"You go to Intercontinental Insurance today and see Luigi Manzo," I said. I gave him the address. "He is expecting you. I am going back to America, but perhaps I will see you in about a year. *A rivederci.*"

"A rivederci," he said. He looked as if he were going to say more.

"It is between men," I told him. "There should be no thanks."

I walked out and went back to the car. Piero grinned at me. "Did you get him fixed up?" he asked.

"Yes," I said. I tossed the knife down on the seat beside him. "You can add this to your collection. It hasn't killed anyone and now it won't. Now you may take me to the airport, my good man."

"Yes, master," he said.

When we arrived at the airport, there was just time for us to go into the bar and have a last drink together. Then it was time for me to board the plane. Piero walked with me to the gate.

I remembered something when we got there. I took off my coat, unbuckled the holster, and handed it and the gun to him. "Thanks," I told him. "It saved my life."

"But you didn't kill anyone with it," he said.

"Not anyone," I said. "But if anyone should ask you, that little gun killed a wild boar that weighed almost five hundred pounds. And just in time." I remembered something else. "I was supposed to get a prize of a case of champagne for killing the largest boar. You tell Gambero I want it sent to me."

"I'll do better than that," Piero said. "I'll go out to his place and get the champagne and send it to you myself."

"In that case," I said, "you might slip in a couple bottles of that brandy. And tell Gianna good-bye for me. Tell her I ran into censorship trouble with my movies and I'm out of business."

"I already called her this morning," he said with a grin. "I told her that you had become so fond of wild boar hunting that you had decided to take it up as a career. I am taking her to dinner tonight to console her."

"I knew the minute I saw you that I couldn't trust you," I told him. *"Allora, di nuovo—a rivederci."*

"A rivederci," he said.

I went through the gate and walked toward the plane. For some reason, it seemed like a long, lonely walk.

AFTERWORD

The Wilma Montesi Case

A Lonely Walk, first published in 1956, was inspired by the Wilma Montesi case of 1953, a scandal that rocked Italy with revelations of corruption in high places. Signorina Montesi's death is an unsolved mystery to this day. The case, accompanied by a defamation trial that stretched over several years, was full of juicy details that Ken Crossen must have culled from newspaper reports, since full-length books about it in English did not appear until many years later. Around the facts he wove a characteristic Milo March adventure of exciting exploits, close calls, amusing banter, and sexy interludes. The novel wouldn't be complete without familiar characters like the worldly-wise street urchin, a cooperative policeman (who trades Dante quotes with Milo), a blonde with "all of her assets below her shoulders," and a brunette of equal dimensions but more complex assets above the neck. Milo has said: "I have been known to chase a blonde—when there wasn't a brunette around."

In real life, the young man who was implicated in Wilma Montesi's death (but not prosecuted), was a prominent politician's son known as "the blond." No doubt that is why one of the characters in *A Lonely Walk* is named Gianna Bionda, whose last name means "Blondie." The real-life blond man's name was Piccione, which translates as "pigeon," an image that political cartoonists of the day had fun with. In this book, a primary suspect is a young man whose father is a government official and whose name is Balena, which means "whale." Ken Crossen seems to have enjoyed choosing names for his Italian characters, including Coniglio (rabbit), Gambero (crayfish), and Manzo (beef). And one of the main characters in the book is named Wilma, though she's not the victim.

Wilma Montesi

The fictional victim is Anna Maria Pericoloso, whose body—just as in Wilma Montesi's case—is found near a luxurious seaside estate where prominent people are invited to extravagant parties, *La Dolce Vita* style, with plenty of alcohol and a wild-boar hunt. It's impossible for male guests to escape the hunting competition, an obligatory display of virility. Milo, feeling silly, is provided with a hunting coat and utters, "Tallyo and yoicks," before solemnly heading for the woods. He would rather be draped over a barstool, martini in hand, than shooting at a 500-pound pig charging him at full speed. The boar hunt proves to be anything but entertaining for him, but it is surely one of the great Milo moments in the series.

In this story, Milo unexpectedly runs up against his past when he meets a woman who, like him, underwent some rough experiences as an underground fighter in Europe. World War II is something Milo would like to forget, but its staying power in the mind is insistent. Ken Crossen reminds us of how much the world had changed by the mid-1950s. As one character says, "It used to be that there was no doubt about who was a friend and who was an enemy. Today it is not so easy. Everybody is all mixed up with everybody else." And Milo reflects, "It was only a few years since we had fought the great war, but already many of the lines were blurred. It was that way all over the world. When it served their purpose, Fascists and Communists and Democrats might all sit down together, or any two of them team up against the other. Cynicism was once more abroad in the land." In such confusing times, our hero sticks to a simple rule: "There are ideas I dislike and ones that I like. I try to stick to those and to hell with compromising them."

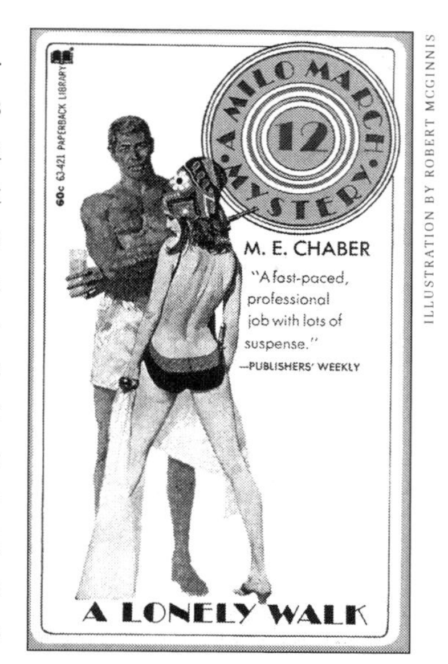

ILLUSTRATION BY ROBERT MCGINNIS

Kendra Crossen Burroughs

ABOUT THE AUTHOR

Kendell Foster Crossen (1910–1981), the only child of Samuel Richard Crossen and Clo Foster Crossen, was born on a farm outside Albany in Athens County, Ohio—a village of some 550 souls in the year of this birth. His ancestors on his mother's side include the 19th-century songwriter Stephen Collins Foster ("Oh! Susanna"); William Allen, founder of Allentown, Pennsylvania; and Ebenezer Foster, one of the Minute Men who sprang to arms at the Lexington alarm in April 1775.

Ken went to Rio Grande College on a football scholarship but stayed only one year. "When I was fairly young, I developed the disgusting habit of reading," says Milo March, and it seems Ken Crossen, too, preferred self-education. He loved literature and poetry; favorite authors included Christopher Marlowe and Robert Service. He also enjoyed participant sports and was a semi-pro fighter in the heavyweight class. He became a practicing magician and had a passion for chess.

After college Ken wrote several one-act plays that were produced in a small Cleveland theater. He worked in steel mills and Fisher Body plants. Then he was employed as an insurance investigator, or "claims adjuster," in Cleveland. But he left the job and returned to the theater, now as a performer: a tumbling clown in the Tom Mix Circus; a comic and carnival barker for a tent show, and an actor in a medicine show.

In 1935, Ken hitchhiked to New York City with a typewriter under his arm, and found work with the WPA Writers' Project, covering cricket for the *New York City Guidebook.* In 1936, he was hired by the Munsey Publishing Company as associate editor of the popular *Detective Fiction Weekly.* The company asked him to come up with a character to compete with The Shadow, and thus was born a unique superhero of pulps, comic books, and radio—The Green Lama, an American mystic trained in Tibetan Buddhism.

Crossen sold his first story, "The Aaron Burr Murder Case," to *Detective Fiction Weekly* in September 1939, but says he didn't begin to make a living from writing till 1941. He tried his hand at publishing true crime magazines, comics, and a picture magazine, without great success, so he set out for Hollywood. From his typewriter flowed hundreds of stories, short novels for magazines, scripts radio, television, and film, nonfiction articles. He delved into science fiction in the 1950s, starting with "Restricted Clientele" (February 1951). His dystopian novels *Year of Consent* and *The Rest Must Die* also appeared in this decade.

In the course of his career Ken Crossen acquired six pseudonyms: Richard Foster, Bennett Barlay, Kent Richards, Clay Richards, Christopher Monig, and M.E. Chaber. The variety was necessary because different publishers wanted to reserve specific bylines for their own publications. Ken based "M.E. Chaber" on the Hebrew word for "author," *mechaber.*

In the early '50s, as M.E. Chaber, Crossen began to write a series of full-length mystery/espionage novels featuring Milo March, an insurance investigator. The first, *Hangman's Harvest,* was published in 1952. In all, there are twenty-two Milo March novels. One, *The Man Inside,* was made into a British film starring Jack Palance.

Most of Ken's characters were private detectives, and Milo was the most popular. Paperback Library reissued twenty-five Crossen titles in 1970–1971, with covers by Robert McGinnis. Twenty were Milo March novels, four featured an insurance investigator named Brian Brett, and one was about CIA agent Kim Locke.

Crossen excelled at producing well-plotted entertainment with fast-moving action. His research skills were a strong asset, back when research meant long hours searching library microfilms and poring over street maps and hotel floorplans. His imagination took him to many international hot spots, although he himself never traveled abroad. Like Milo March, he hated flying ("When you've seen one cloud, you've seen them all").

Ken Crossen was married four times. With his first wife he had three children (Stephen, Karen, Kendra) and with his second a son (David). He lived in New York, Florida, Southern California, Nevada, and other parts of the country. Milo March moves from Denver to New York City after five books of the series, with an apartment on Perry Street in Greenwich Village; that's where Ken lived, too. His and Milo's favorite watering hole was the Blue Mill Tavern, a short walk from the apartment.

Ken Crossen was a combination of many of the traits of his different male characters: tough, adventuresome, with a taste for gin and shapely women. But perhaps the best observation was made in an obituary written by sci-fi writer Avram Davidson, who described Ken as a fundamentally gentle person who had been buffeted by many winds.